Seven Conversations

Nistha Tripathi

FROG BOOKS

First published in India 2014 by Frog Books
An imprint of Leadstart Publishing Pvt Ltd
1 Level, Trade Centre
Bandra Kurla Complex
Bandra (East) Mumbai 400 051 India
Telephone: +91-22-40700804
Fax: +91-22-40700800
Email: info@leadstartcorp.com
www.leadstartcorp.com / www.frogbooks.net

Sales Office:
Unit No.25/26, Building No.A/1,
Near Wadala RTO,
Wadala (East), Mumbai – 400037 India
Phone: +91 22 24046887

US Office:
Axis Corp, 7845 E Oakbrook Circle
Madison, WI 53717 USA

ISBN 978-93-84226-40-4

Book Editor: Anushree Nande
Cover Designer: Sunill Kaushik
Layout: Chandravadan R. Shiroorkar

Typeset in Book Antiqua
Printed at Repro India Ltd, Mumbai

Price — India: Rs 145; Elsewhere: US $6

Dedication

Dedicated to Krsna - I am a speck of you and in me, somewhere you breathe. That is all the identity I could have asked for.

About the Author

Nistha Tripathi likes to write books and software. Her wandering spirit enjoys blogging, traveling, photography and Yoga.

She followed her scholarly pursuits in the United States where she studied MS in Computer Science and dropped out of an MBA program. She worked in Wall Street and New York startups before returning to India to follow her creative passions.

She penned down *Seven Conversations* when she felt that life had given her a story to tell and it was her duty to tell it out loud.

http://www.nisthaonweb.com/blog
http://nisthaonweb.com/blog/seven-conversations/
https://twitter.com/NisthaTripathi

Acknowledgments

I am indebted to my mother for suffering the pain of bringing me into this world, seeing me go far away and then watching me reinvent myself. I hope I can make you proud someday.

"Breathe in experience, breathe out poetry" ~ Muriel Rukeyser

I cannot thank my father enough for passing on to me his writing genes and sense of spirituality, for answering my questions and introducing me to 'faith'. As a girl, I wanted to write a book at some point in life. But he asked me, "What would you write about? You should write when you have lived." I thank him for making me learn the value of patience and experience.

I thank my family (Amma, Didi, Jija ji, Rabbu Dada, Bhabhi, Chuchu and Poochie) for supporting me through light and dark.

I thank Mr. Chowksey and my friends - Prashant and Yaggeta for giving me endless feedbacks and keeping me motivated when I thought of giving up on the story.

I want to acknowledge the influence of Mr. Hukam Gupta who is the most selfless person I know. Thank you for being you.

Dipen Ambalia - How can I thank you enough? You have unconditionally mentored me about the publishing process, I shall never forget it.

"Description begins in the writer's imagination, but should finish in the reader's." ~ Stephen King

Dear reader, I hope I can make you feel what I felt during writing. Thanks for picking up a book from a first-time author. If I had one wish granted, I would want to leave you satisfied.

I sincerely thank Anushree Nande for editing this book and polishing my stones into diamonds.

Special thanks to Sunill Kaushik for designing the book cover and Urvi Dutt for helping with pagination.

Lastly, I thank the Agarwals. Sometimes, all we need to discover new horizons is a little push and you pushed me alright.

Author's Note

You might ask – "Why should I read this? Of all the pointless droll, why?"

To that, let me say this -

We read to occupy ourselves. We read to find respite. We occasionally read to avoid life. A book might even get monotonous - words, countless words, here and there, floating on a page. We read and read on. It becomes a tortuous effort to read anymore but we persist.

And then, it burns. What? The paper of course!

It suddenly bursts into flames. The story sparks itself and we watch. Not because we can watch but because we can't blink. Our eyes dance to the holy dance of words. Words are now singing to us. The story rises gracefully from the flames into a pious *yajna*. A new world emerges and we are shaken out of our stupor. We are now part of that story, dancing along with it. We smile with it and stare in shock of its suspense. That's what a book does to us. We leave a world behind and enter a new one. That's why we read.

Sometimes that world does its own magic on us and we are never the same after having entered it.

I read to catch a glimpse of those worlds. So when I wrote *Seven Conversations*, that is the world I created for you. And, that is why you should read this.

PART ONE

Chapter ONE
When I nearly shot the albatross

Exchange Place waterfront, a place that buzzed with busy footsteps on weekdays, was a land as deserted as the North Pole on that Sunday night. It stood conveniently across a mile wide Hudson River from Manhattan's downtown area. The damp smell of algae from the river, the cucumbery cool breeze and solitude of the starless night was overwhelmed by only one thing - the hefty, sparkling Manhattan skyline. And awe-inspiring it was, subduing the distracting chug of a far-away ferry, the drone of the security helicopters and the whistle of the light-rail.

For a few moments, the sad but steady eyes of the girl standing alone behind the rails sized up those magnificent concrete blocks across the river, decorated with perennial lights that shut out the mighty stars. In her busy but lifeless routine, this act of standing on the boardwalk, leaning against the rails, pausing and looking, held a special meaning - it gave her sanity and strength to live another day.

But tonight, the sight was not enough to heal. She tried to stare harder behind the wisps of her thin brown hair. The buildings faded against her memory of the day. Her marriage and as an extension her life was crumbling apart just as the vision was blurring and breaking down under her silent tears.

Each day had given her one more reason to hate herself and life. *This was not supposed to happen.* Her mind had screamed again and again, day after day and night after night.

The night was grey and the water of the Hudson greyer. It was riding a high tide tonight and the angry droplets of water splashing against the boardwalk sprinkled all over her. Her eyes lowered to the water and the dancing waves that mirrored her own torment. As she stared, the waves reached higher and higher - inviting her for an embrace. It seemed ages since she had been held in an embrace. She did not know how to swim and she wasn't thinking of swimming out anyway.

Her feet started dragging her to the pier that led to the ferry gate. The moss green cardigan fluttered wildly in the wind, against her frail skeleton. She soon stood on the edge of the pier with a gap wide enough for her to slip away and down. This could be her rescue from the insane pain and hurt. She threw aside her flip flops and looked back at the black waters. The flexible pier swayed with the waves under her naked feet.

The dark water billowed and its splashing sound penetrated deep into the girl's heart. It sounded like a hiss of the serpent of fate closing its grip around her. Her eyes no longer blinked. She wouldn't even need to jump since the water touched the pier; all she had to do was step forward. She started to lean in, lifting her foot. Just as she was about to transfer her weight on to the foot reaching out to the water, she was pulled back with a mighty force that made her fall back with a thud.

Her tears had dried away and the midtown skyline with a beaming red Empire State Building dazzled her as soon as her eyes looked up. She was almost blinded - not only by the light but the realisation of the monster that lurked within her. She looked back in alarm at her savior only to find empty space staring back. She circled around in uneasiness but found no one. If it was physically possible, her thumping heart might have exploded out of her tiny chest.

She took a couple of steps back towards the boardwalk and the next moment, her bare feet had started running for her life. She would never forget that night.

Chapter TWO
Leap of Faith

[Two months later]

43m separated Meera from her destiny. It wasn't a race though, it was a fall, a free fall. She was no lover of heights and could not swim, so this was the worst combination of her material fears that she could face in one go. They call it adventure sports but as with most things in life, it was more of a mental battle. Just like the feet don't run the marathon, the arm doesn't throw the shot-put and the fingers don't send the arrow to the bull's eye, the bungee is not performed by anything else but the mind and its determination. To have enough will to come to the jumping platform is half the battle won. But the other half still remains.

The slender figure of Meera Sachdev stood on the Kawarau Bridge in Queenstown, New Zealand. A pleasant breeze blew over the sparkling, turquoise blue water of the Gorge, a color that she had only seen so far in Photoshop. She wore a fitting t-shirt and jeans, and had pinned up her curls in a knot. Her feet were tied together in a leg harness over a layer of towel and a webbing sling backed up by another body harness around the tiny waist. Multiple velcro straps and a daunting cord held her fate. The spectators rustled on her left from the viewing platform at ninety degrees to the bridge she was standing on. The bungee guide started his pep talk and nudged her towards the edge slowly and steadily.

Don't worry, you'll love it. Not a single person has ever regretted doing this. I have done it a hundred times and there's nothing else I still like to do more than this.'

She was not the extreme sports, adventure seeking girl and the reason behind her standing there could be attributed more to a tortured life than to a thirst for thrill. She was called right away for her jump without getting any time to watch the others, and pump herself up. Everything was happening too fast. Before she knew it, she was on the edge standing with tied feet and free hands that were told not to hold on to anything. The climax was approaching and she made that one fatal mistake you are not allowed on that platform - her eyes happened to look down at the gushing water. *Oh, no!* was all that was needed to paralyse her mind into backing out. Her heart was beating faster than that of a mouse.

'Please don't push me, I'm not ready!' she pleaded, holding tightly on to the rail.

'No one will push you, do you want to do it?'

'I want to, but I can't.'

'Yes you can, if you really want it.'

'No, no I can't. I can't even swim,' she said, turning back without giving the guide a chance to respond.

She was moved aside to give the chance to another person behind her. She watched with disappointed eyes as her mind darted back to every single moment that had precipitated her decision to come here and jump off this bridge. Why was she doing it? Because this symbolised conquering her biggest mental block - her fear of free fall and drowning. She had so much going on in life right now that she thought if she could just take this leap of faith, she would be able to defeat everything else too and get over any hurdle in life.

Right from the moment her New Zealand trip got finalised, she had dreamed of this one thing. She stood there thinking about what scared her anyway - death? What could death take away from her at this juncture in life? Yes, she had accomplished nothing of what she thought or wanted, she had not lived enough, not loved enough, not laughed enough - but to preserve her life at the cost of this dream and all future dreams could not be a worthy choice.

Even if something happened to her while jumping, she would have died trying to live her dream. But if she left with this fear unconquered, she would never have the conviction to take any courageous decision ever again. *And she knew what that meant.* Too much was at stake here. So, she made up her mind - she would close this gap of 43m. At any cost.

For the second and last time, she stood at the iconic spot. The tall, big crew leader came behind her and made her stretch her hands out wide and look straight ahead at the gorgeous scenery. Perhaps the Titanic music would have played in the background but she was too focused on accomplishing her goal to notice how beautiful the sky and mountains looked or how loud the spectators were cheering.

'Sweetheart, you can do it and you will remember it forever. Believe me. Just tell me when you are ready,' he whispered in her ears having inched her on to the edge.

'Let go,' echoed her inner voice next.

She took a deep breath, closed her eyes and leaned forward. In two seconds, she was wobbling disoriented in mid-air. As the rope slackened and straightened again and again, she opened her eyes and flashed the most accomplished smile of her life so far.

Our failures damage the temple of our soul by watering the seeds of self-doubt that when germinate around its walls, shake its whole foundation. The overgrowth of weeds had debilitated the temple's existence so much in Meera's case that nothing short of a plunge into the unknown could sever the weed at its roots. The leap had to be taken, the faith had to be reinforced.

Losing the momentum after a few rebounds that seemed like an eternity, she hung upside down like a bat. She could now acknowledge the warmth of the sun, the loveliness of the breeze and awesomeness of the view. She was still smiling when she was pulled down on the boat by the bungee crew. Her heart kept beating. *I did it, I did it.*

The walk up the stairs from the river to the cliff top was the culmination of the celebration, giving her a feeling of having arrived somewhere. Before leaving, she sprang back to the bridge to hug the crew leader who was taken a bit aback at first. But then he hugged her heartily, engulfing her petite frame in his magnificent one.

'Thanks, you pushed me, didn't you?' she asked with a smile.

He winked, 'No push can make you do that if you don't want to. You conquered it! Always remember that.'

She walked off with a newly instilled faith but she knew it was only the beginning of an arduous voyage.

****

[One month later]

The cabin lights were dimmed as the 747 started wheeling slowly for departure. Meera had been on so many of these long flights to India that her body or mind did not register any particular reaction. Besides, she had other things on her mind. She had been silently crying, if there is such a thing, for past few hours. So she was only too happy to be camouflaged in the darkness from her window seat to let some of those tears find a way out. If the Indian monsoon was as perennial as the tears in her eyes these days, India would never have another drought. An accomplished academic and successful professional life had made her think at one point that life is a breeze.

Having come from modest origins, she had risen to good corporate titles and had married at the ideal Indian marriageable age of 26 to a guy with modern outlook. The recipe was set to produce a successful marriage and family. But as some wise person has said, fate is not an eagle, it creeps like a rat. Fate had crept and decided its own course. Meera was leaving behind the life she had carefully sculpted.

The aircraft began to gradually accelerate as the engine's whirring sound kidnapped Meera away from her past for a second. As the wheels finally relinquished the ground, the reality struck Meera - her so-called home for the last eight years was no longer her home. Through her moist eyes, she beheld the colorful bokeh of city lights below. The magnificence of Manhattan had always enraptured her. The city of the rich and powerful. The capitalist capital of the world that was home to some of the world's greatest men and women. The city that rewarded talent and genius.

Meera had always felt privileged to be a part of the concrete jungle that never slept. As the lights of Manhattan's towering skyline receded, her association with anything that could be called her own was vanishing too. Eight years is a long time to make one forget older associations but it is not long enough to form everlasting bonds with a new land. She was too *desi* to ever be happy in a foreign land and she had now become too *firangi* to settle back happily at home.

Leaving unceremoniously like this was no less painful than how she had felt when she left India eight years ago for a foreign land, but this pain was different and scary - it was like a black hole and not a tunnel of darkness that would, at some point, end. When she had left for the unknown earlier, it was a natural unknown course that she had taken up to conquer. But this time, the unknown was not the natural or socially acceptable course. She was going against the tide. The higher the flight was elevating, the deeper her heart was sinking. Literally and metaphorically, she was neither here nor there - she was like a particle floating in space with no gravity to claim it. She could puke but she was too empty inside.

Her tired eyelids tried to find some rest but the tears wouldn't let them close. So she kept staring at the vast expanse of maroon-grey sky outside. It seemed as barren as her own life. The weather outside gradually became rougher and the aircraft was left rocking off and on. The opportunity was well captured by the infants to send out shrill wails that made her realise that it was going to be a long flight. She finally took out her allergy pill to help her fall asleep.

After fourteen long hours, the Delhi city lights had begun to appear below the clouds as Meera glanced from the window. Previously this sight would give her tremendous joy but tonight she was listless if not morbid. Deliberately, she waited till the other passengers cleared out, before leaving the aircraft.

A splash of water can only do so much to bring back some decency to any sad and tired face but she tried before mechanically proceeding through the immigration and baggage collection. There was a time when she had waited hours in the embassy to get the coveted US visa and squealed with joy on seeing that big colorful stamp on her passport. Now, it was no longer valid. No, she could never have imagined that she would be giving it up voluntarily under such circumstances.

Lately, she had developed strong aversion to any company and was eager to get out of the swarming airport. She hadn't brought any gifts for anyone, so the last thing she expected was to be stopped at the customs.

'Madam, ye aapka hai?[1],' said the police woman who was inspecting her hand luggage at the customs check.

'Yes, what is it?' Meera curtly responded.

'Kitni jewellery le ja rahi hain aap?[2]'

It dawned on Meera that she was carrying significant amount of gold and diamond wedding jewellery with her.

'But these were all purchased in India.'

The woman shook her head and called out to one of the older officers on the other side,

'Arre Pandey ji, dekhiye to idhar.[3]'

Pandey ji knew what that meant and beamed with happiness. As he ambled towards her, Meera's heart sank upon realising that she had given the authority a solid chance to extort something out of her. Meera remembered the times she had refused to bring laptops for her cousins because she was against paying bribes to the custom officers. Acquiescing and playing along might have been a wise

---

[1] Madam, is this yours?
[2] How much jewellery are you carrying?
[3] Mr. Pandey, please see this.

thing to do but practicality was never her forte. Instead of letting her better senses prevail, she started grimacing and countering.

This only made Pandey ji more obnoxious.

'Itna gold to Madam allowed nahi hai, ispe to duty lagegi.[4]

'Haan but duty tab lagti agar wo maine US se purchase kiya hota but ye saara India me liya hua hai. Ye meri shaadi ki jewellery hai.[5] And now I am returning to India, so bringing everything back. Why will I pay anything on the jewellery bought in India?'

Pandey ji was neither interested in her marital status nor used to hearing such tones, so he just leaned back on his chair and said casually,

'Theek hai to receipt dikha do.[6]

Meera replied in a low tone that belied utter rage,

'Sir, *ab receipt abhi to hai nahi mere paas*[7], it's been three years.'

Pandey ji was of course waiting for such lack of preparation,

'Koi baat nahi, hum bag yahan pe rakh lete hain, jab aap receipt le aaoge tab le jaana.[8]

Yeah right, I am leaving all that with an asshole like you here, thought Meera.

Thereupon, *Pandey* ji went on a stroll and the lady police officer came closer to Meera. Looking at her doubtfully and then double checking that she was traveling alone, she asked,

'Aap married ho?[9]

Meera was flabbergasted and wanted to scream, *What the fuck, none of your business!* but uttered a quiet *'Haan'.* She knew

---

[4] Madam, so much gold is not allowed, you'll need to pay the duty on this.

[5] Yeah but that would be so if I had purchased this jewellery in US but I have bought this in India. It is my wedding jewellery.

[6] Ok then show us the purchase receipt.

[7] I don't have the receipt.

[8] Not a problem, leave the jewelry and we will release it when you show us the receipt.

[9] Are you married?

she was going to have to answer that question a lot of times in the future.

'*To pehen ke aana chahiye tha na Madam, itni jewellery aise kyon carry kar rahe ho?*[10]'

Meera was about to reply, *Yeah, of course, I should be wearing this three tier gold necklace with my jeans,* but refrained.

'*Aap log please mujhe pareshan mat kijiye*[11], just look at this jewellery, you can tell from the design that it is made in India', she tried to appeal to an invisible sense of righteousness among the officers.

She waited twenty minutes with no response. Her puckered eyebrows and creased temple gave the only human touch to an otherwise lackadaisical face.

Afterwards, out of the blue, an officer came towards her who had been watching the whole scene.

'*Itna gold leke nahi ghoomna chahiye na aapko,*[12]' he said in a stern but polite tone.

'I know, I'm sorry but *mere circumstances hi kuch aise the!*[13]' she almost choked up.

The officer looked at her penetratingly and asked the lady police to let her go. Meera took her bag gracefully and looked at the eyes of the officer who had just let her off the hook and said, 'Thanks, I really appreciate it.' She gathered her luggage and strolled slowly to the gate.

She had finally arrived in India.

Dread would be an understated expression for Meera's state of mind as she anticipated the look on the faces of her parents

---

[10] Why are you carrying so much jewellery in the bag? You should have worn it instead.
[11] Please don't harass me.
[12] You shouldn't be carrying so much gold.
[13] My circumstances were so.

who must have been waiting to receive her. The humid gust of wind kissed her as she stepped out. The hustling bodies, wheat complexions and commotion on the porch were all too familiar and dear to her - anything that she associated with India was all too dear for her. In between the heads in the crowd, she spotted her father - as composed and serene as ever. There was no jumping or waving, just an acknowledgment and relief.

But she couldn't help cringing when her mother embraced her without saying a single word. She hugged her for more than 5-6 seconds that seemed like an eternity in heaven. As she pulled back to face her mother, she had fortunately managed to find her long lost smile but something else had accompanied it - few tears in her eyes. Her mother kissed her on the forehead and said, '*Aa gayi beta*[14]' so gently that for a moment, the order of whole universe seemed restored to Meera.

She wondered how there could be anything wrong as long as one had their mother to come back to. As this emotional reunion overwhelmed her vulnerable state of mind, her consciousness found a way out of her hold just as a dying person's last breath tries to escape their ailing body - she fainted. The last sound in her ears was a suppressed scream from her mother.

---

[14] You have come, my dear.

Chapter THREE

Storm and Stress

'I never liked her. All those questions. She wasn't here to see how Meera is doing, she was here to make sure the situation is as bad as she had heard,' Meera's mother, Amrita, gushed her uninhibited comments on the latest visitor.

'Her false consolations! What impudence! Did you see how affected she was sounding?' Amrita then began her attempts at mimicking her guest - 'Oh *bhabhi*, I did not sleep for many nights when Manu told me. I just could not believe. Meera is so sensible, she can never take a wrong decision.'

Her monologue continued, 'Sleep! What does she know about sleep? I never liked her, never!'

'Amrita, you are exaggerating. Please calm down,' said Sumer. He paused and continued, 'This was going to happen and we knew it. You can't shut people up.'

The conversation floated through the air to the adjoining room where Meera was supposed to be asleep. The doctor had advised her bed-rest since last week. Her protests held little meaning after how she had collapsed at the airport. Sleep was never a problem with her before. Well, the remarkable thing about sleep is, it always comes uninvited and unwanted. But upon invitation, it transforms into that mirage which draws away further, even as it draws you on. And then there's the fact that misery and sleep are like the moon and sun - rarely visible simultaneously. While keeping strong bondage with misery these days, Meera had seen increasing little sleep night after night.

There had been a steady flow of visitors who came to see Meera, mostly family, strictly controlled by her mother. No one in her family had been divorced in the known past, so there was no precedence or accepted norms for such a visit. Consequently, comments and expressions varied. Not a single person had said the most obvious thing on their mind - "Are you kidding us?" but they had been blatantly incompetent at hiding it. Indians, as a race, are well-accomplished liars when it comes to stating hurtful opinions. But having arrived from a country where frankness is encouraged right from childhood, Meera hated when her guests consoled her with fake do-not-worrys. Lately, she had even stopped responding and sometime resorted to fake sleepiness when conversations started becoming awkward.

After so many depressing encounters and sleepless nights, Meera's capacity to absorb any more grief was no more than that of a saturated sponge's ability to soak more water. So, her parents' concerned conversations passively registered in her mind without causing any visible deterioration for now, but were certain to come back haunting as and when her mind became fit to be harmed. She welcomed the numbness.

You can feed a canary in a cage and make her healthy but the soul never learns the music it doesn't want. Thus, Meera healed and regained some of her lost kilos. Her brain also, one can argue, started to become un-numbed and absorb the queued molecules of sorrow. The healthier she was being forced to become, deeper was the awareness of her afflictions. Every hushed voice upon her arrival and every consolation kept adding to her desolation. Not everyone mattered but the hardest hitting part was the look of doom in the eyes of her well-wishers. They looked at her with concealed pity as if she was suffering from a terminal disease. Gradually, life started to move on.

****

A couple of days later, she was visited by someone she was happy to see for a change.

Charu hugged Meera tight. No opening words were necessary.

'I wish you had told me earlier.'

'I didn't know it would come to this,' Meera confessed.

'I can understand. It doesn't matter now. If you have taken it, then it must have been the right decision,' Charu added.

'God, I missed you so much. You are a sight for my sore eyes. There was no one to talk to. And then, towards the end, it happened all too soon. Once I realised it was over, I just couldn't breathe there anymore.'

Meera's face turned more animated than it had been in months. Her eyes went off somewhere far and all the suppressed grief came floating up to her visage.

'Let's go,' Charu said abruptly.

'Go? Where?' Meera asked with an impatient look that was hoping for only that answer in which she did not have to go anywhere.

But Charu had already made up her mind and was standing now, 'Coffee or something. Just get up.'

'I just had coffee.'

'Would you just get up?' Charu had the ability to make her eyes wider and bigger whenever she wanted to get something done.

Meera did not know what had precipitated so suddenly, so she quietly obeyed.

'Now, don't keep standing here...go change that ghastly shirt of yours. And no slippers!'

Meera stubbornly sat down again, 'I'm not going anywhere, definitely not changing for it.'

But Charu had pulled her hands and got her back up on her feet quite easily.

'You know I won't be the first to get tired of your childish game. So, show that sensible self of yours and don't delay.'

Meera gave up and went in but not without showing her displeasure. When she returned, she found Charu happily chatting with her mother. Meera remembered how Charu could coax anyone especially parents into saying yes. Even in college, Meera was never allowed any sleepovers at friends' places except for Charu. Clearly, she had not lost her charm.

'No worries beta, go wherever you like. If you bring a little smile on her face, you come to me whenever you want that favorite *bhutte ka kees* of yours,' Amrita was saying.

'Even out of season?' Charu replied quickly to which Meera's mom could only struggle to answer.

'Kidddddding aunty,' Charu hugged her tightly, '*Ab to Meera ko hansaana hi padega!*[15]

Meera's mom smiled in that sweet way Moms smile when they are brimming with love. 'God bless you' was all she could manage.

Meera opened the car's front door and sat inside, 'Okay, what's the idea?' she looked inquiringly at Charu who looked all set to drive the hell out of the city today.

'Idea is to remind you what good times are,' said Charu with a smile and understanding that only a close friend can boast of.

Meera sat silently just tracking the route her abductor was taking. Soon, they were walking through the front door of Paparazzi, the new five-star in town.

'Don't you think I'm a little under dressed for this?' said Meera looking at the glittering lobby.

'Who cares? Anyway, it will look cool, as if you don't care where you are. And do speak in that *firangi* accent of yours!'

Charu flashed a charismatic smile.

---

[15] Now I need to make Meera smile.

'Now this isn't New York, so you'll have to do with whatever is available.'

'I will try.'

Minutes later, they were seated at the club lounge area near the pool.

'Impressive, how did we find a seat so fast?' Meera enquired of her companion after noticing a stuffed waiting anteroom on their way in.

'You are with a person who holds a certain reputation in media circles. And hotels like to treat media people nicely. It doesn't hurt to have some big profile interviews taking place in your lounge or get some extra coverage in case of events. You know.'

'Charu Saxena, look at you! The girl who would just not keep quiet, who always dreamed big and here you are. You know I'm totally envious right now,' Meera flashed a genuine smile.

Meera was still appraising the posh interiors and seemingly elite society diners who were boozing with sophistication when she heard Charu already commanding the waiter, 'Two Jack Daniels. Neat.'

'Whoa, Charu, no. I'm not drinking.'

'Relax, I know you don't drink but maybe its time for an exception.'

'Well, I did drink at times but...'

'Wha! I can't believe Meera Sachdev drinks!! That's so not like the well behaved girl we know you are!' Charu had cut her short and had flung her hands in the air, throwing a charade that could fool anyone but her friend.

'*Kya kalyug aa gaya hai. Mira Bai ne bhi peena shuru kar diya!*[16] Remember how half the class had started calling you Mirabai after that English play we read?'

---

[16] What a kalyug, even Mirabai has   started drinking.

A couple of heads had turned in their direction at this out-of-place comment.

'Shut up drama queen! And for God's sake, hush!' Meera pretended to scold her.

'*Ab to mujhe do peg lene hi padenge*[17],' Charu had exclaimed as the waiter just arrived with their drinks. Her statement made the waiter ask, 'Shall I bring some more?'

'Yes sir, please. One for me seeing my friend after a long time. One for me realising that she is already a *piyakkad*[18]. And one for her - though I'm not sure if just one will even wet her tongue,' Charu replied playfully.

Meanwhile, Meera had picked up the glass in front of her to take a sip. 'Not bad'.

The next sip was several magnitudes larger and can be better termed as a gulp. It had been a long time since she had attended a happy hour, and with her best friend in front, she thought it was time to relive some memories.

'Yes, one more please,' Meera interjected as she gulped the remaining content of the glass. She continued, 'Do you have sake?'

'Yes ma'am, we do.'

'Perfect, get that too. Two.'

'That's my girl!' Charu applauded.

The people who had interested themselves in the affair of two girls, seemed to have realised that it was nothing more than two habitual drunkards enjoying their celebratory libation, and had gone back to the delicacies that sought their attention with greater urgency.

The cheers followed with paused sips, gulps and appetizers one after another. Meera began narrating the miserable story of

---

[17] Now I need to get two pegs.
[18] Drunkard.

her marriage with suitable participation from her listener. Charu had cautiously refrained from asking delicate questions or making comments that could invite any negative thoughts.

'I don't know how I survived that time. There were moments when I would start walking and the river looked too inviting. Days and nights were like an imprisonment except that the jail was not locked and there was nothing outside that would make me want to flee. So, I would remain there, paralysed in a way but not knowing that I was paralysed. My words must be making no sense right now,' said Meera with a weak smile.

Charu did not speak or blink for sometime. It was not often that she was at a loss of words. Finally, she rested her hand on Meera's and managed to find a voice, 'Sweetheart, good to have you back. That is not a life worthy of you. Frankly, when I got the phone call from your Mom, I was worried. I wanted to talk to you to confirm that your decision wasn't an impulsive one. I know you but when it comes to matters of the heart and life, emotions can interfere with the sanity of any person, even one as discerning as you are. I am glad we talked. I don't even know how to tell you without sounding like I'm consoling, but you are one hell of a girl. To marry a guy against your parents' wishes and then sanely accept the circumstances that followed is not easy. Then, you had the courage to realise that maybe the marriage was not working, your decision was not working. But you did not stick to it, which would have been convenient, you chose to move on and work for your happiness. Not many people can do that.'

'I don't know and I don't care. I'm sure I was a bitch too. In fact, I know I was. Just wasn't working, *yaar*.'

'Great. So, you really did bungee jump?'

Meera nodded, 'And that day I knew, I would not quit on myself. I announced to D that I was calling the marriage off the very week that I came back from New Zealand. Frankly, if I had failed to do the bungee jump, I would never have had the courage to take such a step. Three years of misery and failure had rendered me,' she paused to find the right word, 'Useless.'

'Well, I think we should celebrate, because for all we know, that river might have claimed you in some moment of desolation and we would have been left crying for rest of our lives.'

Meera knew the message Charu was trying to convey under the mask of humour. She smiled, 'Don't worry, I'm not suicidal.'

'You better not be!'

'I'm really glad you could come on such a short notice. When are you leaving for Singapore?'

'This weekend. But when I come next time, we should talk about how Professor Bakshi had a soft corner for you.'

'No, he didn't!'

The tales were told and happy times relived late into the night.

The house was quiet when Charu dropped Meera off in an inebriated but happy state. She tiptoed straight to her bedroom upstairs.

****

Meera got up early the next morning and came down the stairs feeling more cheerful than she had felt ever since coming to India. The living room was empty and she could hear murmurs outside in the verandah. The golden sunrays lighting the front door brought a subtle smile to her face. She realised how having tea out in the garden on chilly winter mornings was one of her favorite memories about this house. She moved ahead, looking forward to reliving it, but hearing the bits of conversation outside made her pause.

Meera's mother was softly saying, 'I can't see her like this, Sumer.'

'You think we should start looking for a suitable groom?' he hesitatingly asked.

'I am not sure. I don't know if she is ready. She looks so weak, I have never seen her like this before.'

Amrita's words came haltingly, 'She was the strongest kid in the family, wasn't she?'

'Yes, she was.' He added, 'She still is.'

'I'm really afraid for her. This world is not very forgiving, our society does not forget things easily. I hate to admit it but I don't see how she is ever going to be happy again,'

'How I wish things could get better without a divorce but that is out of the question now. It is out of question, isn't it?'

'Of course it is, Sumer!' Amrita said in an outraged manner. 'I'm never letting her go back into that hell.'

There was a long pause.

'And if we file for separation, the case is not going to be over anytime soon either. I don't know if I have it in me anymore to fight. I feel tired and helpless.'

'You know what hurts me most? That she may never find the love she deserves, she may never be able to love again. Her...her marriage may never turn out like it should. This life is too long to lead a solitary life and yet I don't know if it's worse than an unhappy marriage.'

'Let's not be so negative. Come, I'll make some *pudina* tea for you.'

Meera hurried back upstairs to her room as soon as she heard the approaching footsteps of her Dad. All the barriers that she had put against negative and depressing thoughts over the last few weeks had fallen in one blow. The infinite capacity we have to fight the challenges in life evaporates away in a jiffy when it's our parents standing on the suffering end. Seeing her Dad stand helpless had obliterated all the happiness and optimism she was feeling last night - the illusion created by alcohol was over and she was back to the cruel reality. She was a failed woman - at relationships, at life. And she was unemployed, sad and lonely. On top of that, she was the cause of misery for her parents. Was there any reason left to be still living?

Chapter FOUR
One: Conversation of Pain

Meera splashed cold water on her face and looked at her reflection in the mirror. It was just too hard to not ask herself, *What do you think you are doing?* or *Why can't you just lead a normal life?* The answers rolled down slowly from her eyes. She closed her eyes and turned away from the mirror. She might have alleviated deeper confrontations for now but she knew that she needed those answers - not for anyone else but for herself.

She locked her room gently and leaned back on the door. The grief was making her so miserable that she feared she would collapse if she started crying. She clenched her fists, closed her eyes and tried to black everything out in a desperate attempt to not lose her composure. It was in moments like these that she would think of Krsna. When she did not know where else to turn to, she would summon her savior. It was a technique she had adopted in her last months in New York because frankly, dire times call for dire measures. The habit had incepted one night in New York when she just couldn't sleep. She had closed her eyes and was trying to find something to focus on. She began trying meditation but soon realised that her mind fluttered more than the wings of a butterfly. Unconsciously her thoughts would drift to her past, her failures and her angst. And what was the point in trying to meditate when all you can feel is anger and revolt? So, she resorted to the mundane practice of picturing something that you can concentrate on. She searched her life and past for anything that she could cling on to for support and which was grand enough to contain her. Sifting through objects, people and places, she came to the thought of Krsna - the mysterious, complex and consummate incarnation of Lord Vishnu. While Ram had always generated immense faith in her, Krsna had intrigued her. She could worship Ram - Ram was an ideal human and king, she could understand Ram and see him do the right thing but Krsna was beyond right and wrong as perceived by mere mortals, Krsna was incomprehensible and above her sensibility, Krsna could nurture and destroy when needed, Krsna was profound - Krsna attracted her. Yes, she believed she could collect and focus her thoughts on Krsna.

Trying to visualise Krsna was not easy either. She did not want to picture him as any image she had seen of him - she wanted him to morph out of her consciousness and not from the pen of any artist. She wanted to discover him.

That night was mostly spent in a chaos where Meera tried to tie her anxieties to an invisible mortar. She tried but could not ascribe any form to Krsna, she still saw nothing but black expanse. However, she succeeded in turning her mind's eye on a vague but comforting awareness that Krsna was there with her on that forlorn night. And as Ra, the solar deity of light inevitably conquers Apophis at the onset of dawn, so did she manage to find her way out of the night by chasing her yet-to-emerge Krsna.

As expected in a tiresome, flailing and bitter relationship, situations that demanded such rendezvous with the dark savior in the dark hours presented themselves often.

As a result, Meera started finding her comfort evolve in the dark meandering roads through what was sometimes the grove of holy basil, sometimes the banks of Yamuna and sometimes the unknown. Once her awe of his godhood subsided, she started to interact with her nebulous Krsna. Gradually, she was also able to detach her mind from the scene - become an external observer and watch herself roam around him and trying to reach him. It was like her cognisance was dictating her movements within the *bhoomi* of this spiritual plane, as opposed to how the external objects dictates one's action in the outer world. Unfortunately, her consciousness could not dictate what Krsna was doing. It used to be one way conversations where she would describe her sadness and feelings to Krsna who was sometimes meditating in the center or sometimes standing on an empty battleground. In some moments of helplessness and bafflement, she had even hurled her questions at him – *Why me? What did I do to deserve all this?* No answers or reactions ever came back. Weirdly, it still did not feel weird.

As her present pandemonium got better of her sensibility, Meera sat down on the marble floor. It was December and the floor was cold. She folded her feet in *padmasana* and closed her eyes. After counting her slow breaths for a few minutes, the imagery began to unfold in her mind just as the curtain rises from the stage.

The scene was illuminated to show a vast piece of parched land with a huge banyan tree in the middle on a cloudy dusk. It was a flourishing green tree with a multitude of roots hanging all around. The trunk of the tree possibly extended wider than the arms length of 20-25 men. She then saw the side profile of Krsna emerge to the right of the tree - today again, he was sitting in *dhyaan mudra*. All that was perceptible was the trademark yellow dhoti and glitter of pearls and gold adorning his brawny torso. The fireworks of the fluttering *morpankh* and dhoti against his midnight-sky skin dazzled her from afar.

Meera timidly sat down a few feet away from the base of the banyan tree and watched as his aura started to become more distinguished against the setting sun. She had often complained to him of her sorrows but today her heart was not anxious - it was sad. For months, she had stood tall in the face of adversity but after seeing the suffering her actions had inflicted upon her parents, she found herself breaking apart. In this sadness, she murmured with moist eyes, 'Why am I in so much pain, Keshav?'

What happened next electrified her.

The head of the brawny, dark bodied Krsna had turned sideways to look at Meera. She still couldn't see the details of his face due to the radiance it was emanating, but she was aware of his powerful yet kind gaze. A strong tingling sensation swept through her body. Krsna was now speaking to her and his reply was curt - *'Because you still seek happiness externally, you are driven by your senses. You are chasing material pleasures while true happiness lies within. Look into yourself and find the truth.'*

Meera's eyes unwillingly opened and her trance was broken. She was gently trembling - not out of a chill or fear but out of the surmount excitement that had run through her nerve centre. Every cell in her body was on fire. As she blinked arrhythmically, the reality dawned upon her - she had just discovered a connection with Krsna and the fool that she was, she had let it break! In her wretched miserable existence, this one moment could be called divine and she had let it slip away. 'There is no end to my misfortunes, is there?' - she asked herself openly in the stillness of her room.

Her next, immediate instinct was to close her eyes and find that ground and tree again. She hoped her affliction and self-realisation would spark a second chance at divine mercy. As if her mind was trying to rewind a tape that did not exist, the empty reel kept whirring in her head. When nothing came up, her mind even tried to forge the whole scene, but to no avail. There was no Krsna anymore. Ultimately she gave up, leaned back and sprawled herself out on the floor. She fell asleep and to her consolation, this was the best and most peaceful sleep she had gotten in a long, long time.

When she woke up in half an hour, it seemed like an era had passed by. Her hands were not trembling anymore and her body temperature seemed to have come down to normal. She sat back up and replayed the events of the past hour in her thoughts.

'No, it wasn't a dream,' she assured herself.

****

That night before sleeping, Meera picked up a pen and opened her diary.

I think I saw Krsna or felt him. I am not sure...

Chapter FIVE
Life moves on

The life started dragging on and Meera's determination, optimism - whatever was left of it, whatever she had gathered carefully for a heyday - started eroding like an exposed cliff tormented by overpowering waves. Hardly a day passed when she did not witness the pouring of the fountains in her eyes, sometimes during the shower, sometimes just before she fell asleep and sometimes at hours as thoughtlessly chosen as those by a newborn to cry.

The word 'social' finds its roots in Latin word sociālis which means companionable. We are social animals who seek approval and conformation by those around us. Seeking divorce is one of those taboo behaviors that go against the accepted practices and in some religions, even against the God. Not sure if they took God's permission for it but that's what they profess. Having initiated the call for divorce herself, Meera was carrying a burden of responsibility lest her call be one of a misjudged nature. That burden was only growing heavier through time and the judgment of people around her. Every time someone asked her, "Have you made up your mind?" or "Are you sure?" she would internally bleed. How can anyone be sure? The only way to be sure is to live through it, but who will then pay the price of being wrong? Certainly not the people who were questioning her today.

Fortunately, the fantastic nature of the Krsna incident took her mind off those grey thoughts - at least for a while. It had also given her a support to lean against; she took it as a seal of approval that she was on the right track. Why? Because when she asked the real question about why she was in pain, she got an answer which was NOT - "Because you fucked up". That was enough for her. And the one who gave that answer was someone she could put her trust in. She was willing to take that chance anyway.

****

Meera hadn't draped a saree in three years, so when she tucked the final fold with her tenth or eleventh pin, she was nervous. She brushed her hair and powdered her face gingerly. In the mirror, she saw a woman - not charmingly beautiful but gracefully decent. That is more than what she had hoped for. She couldn't remember the last time she looked so mature. Perhaps there was none to remember.

She was soon standing in the auditorium at her college where she was about to give a lecture on 'successful careers' recounting her professional journey in the United States. She finished the presentation she had prepared along the expected lines - how should a student look at his academics, what are the different career options, what to do and what not to do. But then she felt there was something missing.

Just as she was about to wrap it up, she switched the projector off and looked back at her audience with a grave expression. Somewhere in between that crowded auditorium, she saw herself ten years ago - a sincere girl in plain *salwar kameez*, listening intently and trying to work hard towards her dreams. To make it big in life, to earn a handsome salary, to own a luxury car, to live in a big bungalow - isn't that what one was supposed to be dreaming about? And then she thought of moments that had mattered to her most. Yes, that first paycheck was so exhilarating and she had even worked her way to big things that she dreamed about. But she left all that without a second thought when the time came.

She continued, 'Career and job are important in their own ways but life is life. No amount of professional success can fill an empty life. So, seek happiness in your work because that's the highest reward. And only you can know what makes you happy, so don't let someone else decide your path, your future, your destiny. You need to know what you should be doing and then you should have the courage to do it.'

The auditorium had suddenly become very silent and the tired students, alert.

'You know success cannot be pursued. It has to be a by-product of doing things that you love - things that make you happy. Steve Jobs rightly said that you cannot connect the dots looking forward. It can only be done backwards. And, you have to trust that the dots will somehow connect in your future. You have to trust in something - your gut, destiny, life, karma, whatever. You have to believe in magic and that you are meant to do great things. If you remember one thing from this lecture, let it be this - true success is not defined by money or titles, it is measured by happiness. Find out what makes you happy and do it.'

The students applauded heartily.

She came back home a happier person. As she was removing her earrings, her eyes accidentally caught Amrita looking at her wistfully in the mirror. Neither of them said a single word but the communication was instantaneous. Meera was the only child, the bearer of the great expectations of her parents. She was the brightest one in the extended family and had never stood second to anyone. Everything she did elevated her higher until her marriage. And the higher she was, the tougher the fall. That which matters the most, often breaks you the worst.

Meera remembered the times Amrita had sobbed, wishing Meera had been born as a son instead. Seeing her grown up daughter looking lovely in a saree, but leading such a lonely life must have broken her. Amrita blinked first and repeatedly at that to dry out the tears that were accumulating. She hurried to leave, 'I'll go and see to the *dal*.' Meera closed her eyes when she left and kept standing for a long time - she was too paralysed to continue.

Chapter SIX
Rum and Raisin

The night was silent except for the persistent humming of the electronic devices and occasional howling of a stray dog. Meera slept like a soldier on a watch, with closed eyes and a restless mind. Thoughts, worries and doubts had been her constant companions since last couple of years and not the ones she had any control over. True solitude vanished the moment they decided to overtake her, like sunflowers wither when night picks up its darkness and gloom. The more she wanted to leave them behind, the stronger they seemed to cling on. Off late, she could feel their weight in every step. They lived in her and thrived on her like a tumour. From the moment she lay down at night to her entering into true oblivion of sleep, the worries preyed on her mind for minutes and sometimes, hours. In this comatose state, her thoughts often created webs of delusions and manifested themselves in specters and if fortunate, reveries.

She was entangled in one such excursion that night. She was driving along a cliff alone in a convertible. The wind was hurling her hair back and her foot was pressing the accelerator slowly but steadily. She was chasing a group of people who appeared to be at the far end of the mountain separated by curvy sinuous roads. Despite speeding up, the distance did not fade and her anxiety grew as she found that she may never be able to close the gap. She was moving but not advancing. Then she felt a quiver. Her car had started trembling - slow at first and then hard. The cliff was giving away and boulders falling down. Her mouth opened to scream but no sound came out.

With a jerk, her eyes opened and she felt her pillow vibrating. She got up and lifted the pillow to find her cell phone buzzing.

It was a reminder alarm that said - 'D's birthday'. She froze and kept looking at the animated cell phone before gathering herself together to shut it off. She huddled in bringing her bent knees closer to her chest and sinking her face deeper in her arms. Of all the manifestations of her surrendering to a fate stronger than her will, this said the most. As she closed her eyes, she remembered how that alarm usually reminded her to buy rum and raisins for the rum cake.

Rum cake. The traditional dessert she would prepare on her husband's birthday. Her eyes were moist. She tried to think about the last time when her life seemed normal. It seemed like a former life. Every living memory of her happier relationship days was a part of an unreachable past now. The river of doubts between her past and present had flooded, submerging the bridge of the love that connected them. Her eyes neither shed a tear nor blinked. She barely moved, just turning her head sideways to rest her cheek on her knees and look at some distant point behind the wall. She was enduring life; whatever was remaining of it. Mother Teresa once said, "The most terrible poverty is loneliness." By those standards, Meera was the most wretched and destitute soul that breathed in that dark hour of the night.

When she got up the next day, to her disappointment, the night had done little to avert her thoughts away from the significance of that date. She was not even in a state to try fending off any memories. The thoughts of little gatherings with friends, the warm and sweet smell of fresh cake coming out of the oven and the icy chill in the air had all come back to haunt her. She was at first disturbed and then she grew restless; the most natural bit was missing from the memories. Wasn't it about D? It was his birthday and that cake was for him - so, where was he in these memories? Why was her mind not thinking about how he ate the first piece, how they had dinner together...no, there was no personal thought of him and her.

For the first time, she realised that her mind had begun selectively blocking off certain memories. Secondly, there were not many happy memories to block. Of course there weren't, why else would she be here today and not at a grocery store in Manhattan buying rum and raisins? And thirdly, she accepted the fact that a chunk of her life was now lost in a black hole because the only person she shared it with was gone. Some rare moments of laughter, madness, rage, helplessness, hopelessness, cheer, excitement, success, failure - anything and everything – are gone and estranged. She would never find them again - ever. As much as that acceptance hurt, she did not turn her back on it. She thought about it again, slowly and deliberately, to make her mind and heart acknowledge it till the pain subsided into defeat. A defeat because in her younger days, she was naive enough to believe there was nothing that cannot be cured with efforts.

Chapter SEVEN
Two: Conversation of Truth

Uneasiness, melancholy and stress had become the fourth, fifth and sixth members of the Sachdev household. Discussions of lawyers, the state of Meera's marriage or the lack of it and such burdensome topics occupied the minds of the whole family whenever they sat together. Some pains were discussed, some left for more opportune moments that were never to come. Everyone was growing tense and terse, testy and lost.

One day Meera found her parents entertaining a guest, Mr. Shastri who was an astrologer and a palm reader. The purpose soon became clear as she was called in to let him read her hand and birth chart. She acquiesced to please her parents - the least she could do these days. First, the astrologer looked worried and next, Amrita, by looking at his worried face. '*Raahu ki mahadasha chal rahi hai*. No hope for the next 5 years. It is going to be a difficult time.'

Now, even Meera was pissed off - not so much on hearing her doomed fate but that it was going to make her parents more worried if possible. She somehow sat through the next ten minutes during which more morbid stuff was pronounced - 'You will always get smaller results than the efforts you put into anything. You will never get anything from your luck. You have faced a terrible time during last three years but the tide has not turned yet. Keep patience. I will tell you what stone can heal you. First, you should sleep with a *gomed* under your pillow. Then, we'll get you a pearl to wear on your middle finger.'

Meera muttered under her breath, 'How did you know I was thinking about the middle finger too?' The engrossed astrologer might have missed the derision but the same could not be said about Amrita who was looking at Meera sternly yet sadly. Meera averted her eyes quickly on seeing the expression on her mother's face.

Next, he started reading Meera's left hand, switching to her right hand at random intervals. Suddenly, he would twist the palm in weird directions and read some faint line under his magnifying glass. If the situation was less preposterous, Meera would have welcomed the amusement of the process but it only ended up irritating her more. Eventually, she politely but firmly reclaimed her hand and got up, 'Sorry, I have an appointment. I need to go. Nice meeting you.' She left without looking twice at Mr. Shastri or her parents.

****

Next morning, Amrita brought a few pieces of toast to the breakfast table and sat down without uttering her customary Good Mornings. Sumer began to quietly fold the newspaper in his hands as Meera entered with everyone's coffee and placed Amrita's mug in front of her.

'Amrita, I don't feel like eating toast today, do we have some plain bread?' asked Sumer as he looked at the plate that Amrita had brought - the pieces were all too burnt. Amrita continued to mechanically sip her coffee and look afar. Meera gently got up and took the plate inside the kitchen. She returned with a few slices of plain bread and butter.

'Amrita!' exclaimed Sumer with a worried voice that broke Amrita's trance.

'What happened?'

'Nothing, put aside the newspaper. Have your breakfast first.'

Amrita extended her hand towards the plate and asked, 'Where is the toast? Wait, let me get some more.' Without giving anyone a chance to respond, she got up and went inside. Meera hurried behind her and caught her staring at the pieces of hard black toast. Before Meera could say anything, Amrita had started sobbing.

'Oh, come Ma, it's not a big deal. I'll put some more in the toaster,' said Meera advancing to embrace Amrita.

'Yeah and what about your life? Where do I put that to fix it?' said Amrita, trying to wipe off her tears with her *dupatta*.

'What rubbish are you talking, Amrita?' interjected Sumer from behind. He had just arrived at the kitchen door.

Meera stepped back and leaned against the granite platform. She gently wiped her own eyes and said in a calm voice, 'Why are you making it difficult for me? Why don't you say what's going on in your head instead of killing me like this every day?'

Sumer spoke first, 'Meera *bete*, please go out. Let me talk to your mother.'

'No! I'm not going anywhere, please talk in front of me so that I can know what's going on!'

He became silent for a moment before nodding. 'Yes, you are right.'

Meera was no longer holding back her tears and her voice trembled, 'I'm not dying so much at my misfortune as I am on seeing you guys suffer like this. Why are you treating me like I'm dead? I'm not dying. I could fight the world but I can't fight you. Don't you understand that?'

Her eyes and voice pleaded in a way that made Amrita collect herself together.

Amrita said, 'I just can't see you like this anymore. I try to find good things for you but everything turns bad. I called Shastri ji in the hope of seeing something good in your future but you don't cooperate. I'm not blaming you if you don't trust it, but tell me what to do so I can help you.'

'Shastri ji! You know I would believe in him for your sake but just tell me one thing,' continued Meera in an enraged manner, 'Did he tell you earlier that I would get divorced? Did he tell you how hellish my life was going to be? If not, then don't ask him to look at my future now! Where were your astrologers when everything was going well in my life? No one predicted a nightmare, did they?'

Amrita closed her eyes knowing that Meera was right. Meera walked up and held her by her shoulders. 'Ma, I don't care what any damn astrologer thinks because he doesn't suffer when I suffer. I'm worried about and care about what you think, what Papa thinks. That is all I care about. And if you still trust your daughter, don't be defeated. I can fight all this if you are with me. Don't make me weak. Please.'

'No one is making you weak, darling. Who can make you weak? You are our star!' said Sumer.

A long pause ensued where their eyes did all the talking. Meera looked steadfastly at Sumer until the anxiety and worry in his eyes dismantled. He gently nodded; his face once again donning his trademark calm and confidence. Meera, then, looked at Amrita and smiled. It was harder to wipe worry off of her mother's face, so she just hugged her gently. Sumer stepped in to hug them both in a protective embrace - almost in a ritual that would cast away all the individual tensions and bond them in a oneness that refused to surrender to any naysayer.

****

During the dinner that night, Sumer suddenly proposed that all of them visit the Kaalbhairav temple on Chhatarpur road.

'Let's go for the *suryodaya darshan*[19]. Meera, you should see it, darling.'

Meera, having no particular affinity or hostility to the suggestion, mumbled, 'Sure.'

---

[19] sunrise prayers

Sumer and Amrita were a spiritual as well as religious couple. Living with simplicity and devotion and seeking enlightenment underlined most of their decisions. They considered themselves good Hindus and tried to follow religion as much as possible without going overboard. Most of their family trip destinations were decided based on the significance of the temples in that area. Needless to say, Meera had visited most of the famous temples India had to offer. Although being only a child then, she did not remember half of them. She had already seen the four sacred pilgrimage destinations of Hindus by the time she had turned twelve - she remembered none of them.

As per the plan, the family got up at four am to bathe and get ready. Meera had already been instructed not to speak to until after the *darshan*. So, silently, using hand signs for any communication, they left for the temple. Driving turned out to be a breeze on the highways that were still dark and relatively unoccupied. They reached the temple around six am, still prior to the dawn. The temple gate was closed and its parking area looked deserted. They parked the car below a giant old *peepal* tree that stood few feet away from the gate. Sumer and Meera strolled to the other end of the grounds where some remote shops were located, dimly lit by yellow bulbs hanging from naked wires - indicating that the morning *pooja* attracted a non-zero if not non-trivial number of devotees. They bought the *pooja tokris* containing flowers, *prasad* packets of sugar lumps, incense sticks and Kaalbhairav's special *prasad 'suraa'* - a bottle of alcohol. In the three different baskets that they bought, the bottles varied from a cheap imitation of Imperial Blue whiskey to *desi sharab*.

The birds gradually started chirping to signal the oncoming dawn. After waiting another fifteen minutes, all of them ambled to the main wooden gate and Sumer knocked on it. His calls were answered by an aged priest who opened the gates slowly with a creaking noise. He said nothing and gestured them to continue to another building inside. They walked up to the base of the main temple building and climbed the stairs. On reaching the top, they saw the statue of a black dog facing the inner sanctum whose doors were open. A younger priest welcomed them inside. He was clad in a black kurta and saffron *dhoti*, a red *tilak* and multitude of rings on his fingers - all with different stones. The idol was different than any Meera had seen before. It showed only the orangish *sindoor* covered head of the deity with two huge, deeply inset, silver eyes. There was a distinct opening between the red lips, the purpose of which was to become clear very shortly.

The *pooja* itself took place quickly as the priest took the baskets and put the flowers in front of the idol. He then collected the liquor bottles and poured out the contents in three different plates. He asked each member to pray to Lord Bhairav to fulfill his or her wishes as he set one plate of *suraa* in the mouth of the idol. With a little tilt, the liquor was absorbed by the idol - an action that was considered akin to acceptance of your prayers by Bhairav ji. The drinking of liquor by the idol had made this temple famous among believers and non-believers so much so that some tourists visited just to witness the extraordinary feat of a stone statue drinking alcohol. It was said that the alcohol remains unaccounted for and is not physically found anywhere on the temple premise. Various explanations are offered by the cynics who reason the phenomenon by capillary action and surface tension. But as it is said, no science can make a staunch devotee question the miracles he wants to believe in.

Meera curiously witnessed the feat herself and was cautioned by her scientific mind to keep away from the topic of magic and miracles. She dutifully bowed her head when her turn came but struggled to come up with a wish. When so much has gone wrong with your life, a 'wish' sounds inadequate. What can you ask for in one or two sentences? She just murmured, 'Dear God, please grant me happiness and peace.'

Bhairav ji is an intense and fear-invoking incarnation of Lord Shiv, regarded highly in *taantrik pooja*. In this form, Shiv consumes alcohol and destroys enemies. Meera was still not sure about the special purpose behind this *pooja* as her father had never shown interest in field of *tantra* before. The priest proceeded to cite how devotees travel from afar just to offer this one morning prayer to Bhairav Baba and how their wishes are fulfilled sooner or later. Meera now regretted not asking for a specific wish instead of a broader happiness and peace - something quantifiable would have been nicer.

As they walked out, Meera asked her father curiously, 'So, what's the significance of this? What does it mean?'

Sumer replied nonchalantly, 'What? It's a ritual, some people believe in it.'

'So, serving alcohol to Bhairav ji will fulfill our wishes?'

'It's not about alcohol, it's his *prasad*. Offering a *prasad* to a deity symbolises your feeling of service towards him, it pleases him. As for your wishes, you sound skeptic. You don't believe it will, do you?'

'Seems a tall order,' accepted Meera frankly.

He chuckled. 'You know, those who don't believe in magic will never see it.'

That made Meera go silent and think. Wasn't it true? In all our pragmatism and scientific bent, we shut ourselves off to phenomenon that we can't explain by our rules. Isn't that the beauty of wonder and magic - to believe in something you can't explain and to enjoy the revelation of it? Isn't it magic that makes a player lagging behind suddenly catch on and turn the game around? Aren't some performances magical? It's the same artist, same song but somehow tonight, he is on fire.

She started voicing her thoughts out loud, 'You know, for that matter, what I ask for is ultimately up to me and how hard I work. If I believe in my prayer, why can't I just make it happen myself?'

'Absolutely, no one has stopped you. Sometimes we lose that inner fire and need a faith or divine intervention to regain it. May be that's what a prayer is,' Sumer said looking at her with a mystical smile.

Meera was mostly silent on the way back, thinking over what her father had said. Somehow, she wanted to believe in that morning's ritual and that it had the power to make her wishes come true. That she had asked for happiness and Bhairav ji had the power to give her that. Yes, why not? She had always been a positive person and it's natural to lose your calm in certain situations as the one she was facing. But above it all, she was a person who loved life and wanted to be happy. Who was stopping her from being happy? And the obviousness of the answer made her smile at herself stupidly. No one was stopping her except, maybe, herself. She was already feeling happier and more at peace than she was earlier.

Well, the ritual does work after all - she thought with a smile whose glimpse was caught by Sumer in the rear view mirror.

Meera hadn't felt this good in a long time and was determined to find more magic in every moment of her life from then on.

'Today's sunrise was beautiful. Maybe that's when the magic started. I shall see the sunrise again tomorrow,' she told herself while going to bed. Somehow in her fired-up state, she could not sleep at all. As the clock struck four, her restless and tired mind made her get up and open the balcony quietly. She stepped out to look up at the starry night. Zillions of stars burned light years away from her. Many new were born every day and many old extinguished forever. And yet, looking from far in this sky, everything remained a mystery. Just like her future. What did it hold? What prospects were to burn brighter and which ones to die out? From the distant present, it all seemed so far and hazy. But then, why should she seek to identify the stars individually when together they formed this magnificent night and illuminated this resplendent sky? Why should we lose today for an unknown tomorrow?

That's when she promised herself that she would just enjoy the 'now' - tonight and forever. Her eyes were closing when the first golden rays hit from the east. But she shook herself to look at the glorious amber ball of fire emerge from the horizon and make its way through its trajectory. How suddenly the sky color changed from grey to pink - God's paintbrush action unparalleled in its movement, grace and dispatch. Yes, this was a divine performance too - a divinity we all forget to recognise in our chaotic lives. With a smile, she went off to sleep.

Chapter EIGHT
WereWoman

Meera was reading the morning newspaper when her phone started ringing - it was an old friend. She hesitatingly answered. For long she had avoided meeting her old friends who were still around. Her present circumstances did not make her feel very social these days, her wounds were still too fresh to be recounted casually in a conversation.

'No, you have to come, we'll come to pick you up,' Vinay insisted. 'It will be fun and no one is going to say anything, you should come, *yaar*.'

'Alright, I'll come and meet you guys there directly,' she succumbed.

'It's good for you,' Meera tried to reassure herself. She knew she should be seeing friends and get back to a normal life but what we know we should be doing isn't often what we want to do and is rarely what we end up doing. She was looking forward to seeing Vinay and did appreciate that he had cared enough to force her to come.

She quietly entered Cafe Pallette and was immediately struck by the myriad paintings and queer ornaments adorning its walls. It was not the most popular place for lunch as one could see; there were only handful of tables engaged. It was fairly easy to spot Vinay and the company occupying the biggest table in one corner. They were her old time friends, the newer faces could be attributed to their spouses and some babies. Meera tried to appear cheerful and suppress the weariness that was weighing her heart down at the prospect of facing people who knew nothing of her misfortune.

She received a mixed reception – Vinay and Ameya were warm while the rest, which included few of her other classmates, were more formal. Their expressions made her feel that they had been briefed by Vinay. She politely asked about everyone, exchanged pleasantries with the newer faces and showered compliments on the babies. No one asked a single question about her past, plans or family. That confirmed her suspicion - they definitely knew.

The conversation hardly flowed and there seemed to be too much effort behind the words that were spoken. When they eventually talked about their college days, it helped everyone settle down.

'Meera, you were the bright one. Always the one to know all the answers,' said Snigdha while fussing over her six month old daughter in her arms. 'I always told Adi that Meera is so lucky to have everything, I wish I was too.'

Everyone at the table was now looking intently at Snigdha. Her unruffled manner as she looked back made it clear that the words were intentional. Meera couldn't think how to respond to the jab so badly disguised as a compliment that she only smiled weakly.

'Here we are, engaged in babies now and look at you - always a career woman! But then I think I am blessed with such a family. How I love spoiling them both!' added Snigdha turning to her husband with a broad smile. She then brought her baby close to her face and rubbed their cheeks together to give her the visual proof of her happiness. Meera ignored the malicious display of affection but her eyes were arrested by the chuckles of the little baby wrapped in cute woollens. She froze as she saw the baby paddling her hands vigorously in excitement. She gently said, 'No, Snigdha, who could be more fortunate than you at this moment?'

It was Snigdha's turn to smile weakly upon seeing her weaponry of words rendered ineffective. Her motherly instincts soon took over as she hugged her daughter close in a genuine embrace. Seeing such a natural flow of emotions in lives of people around her only left Meera's feelings cracked wide open like a muddy stretch devoid of any moisture of happiness. She could barely contain the tears on edge of her eyelids and picked up her phone so that she could excuse herself and look away.

Ameya tactfully interrupted to place lunch orders. Lunch took place quietly without further drama.

****

Despite their best efforts, the conversation could barely be kept astray of common topics of domestication - marriage, children, future - that withered away any leftover courage to appear fine on Meera's part. Her mind had already drifted off and fortunately for the adorned walls had found the perfect refuge in bizarre paintings. Her focus was immediately riveted on a majestic oil on canvas that hung in middle of the opposing wall. It occupied a large portion of it using transparent threads that gave an impression of the canvas floating in the air. The place and angle of tilt was wisely chosen to let the visibility be enhanced by the natural light.

The work itself was magnetic and Meera could hardly take her eyes off it. To a casual glance, the painting depicted two women in two different settings - one wistful and other utopian. A closer scrutiny however, revealed the oneness of the two women. The woman, apparently tied in the earthly sorrows as evident from the chains hanging from her frail wrist and left foot, is looking in through a big hole created by the falling of bricks in between a dilapidated wall. On the other side of the wall, she sees herself in a paradisiacal setting - bathed in sunlight, sitting in a yacht, traveling on sparkling waters towards an endless horizon. Accompanying her on the yacht are other people with calm and happy countenance but no one is looking at each other. As the woman in the yacht looks back to her tormented double - her face is adorned with a childish smile devoid of any regret.

The artist's choice of colors made the subject all the more striking. The world outside and the afflicted woman was painted in violet monochrome and the scene on the other side of the window was done in yellowish-golden tones. The colors magnificently enhanced the contrast and use of monochromes displayed the mastery and confidence of the artist over his talent and subject.

With simple letters, the title of the painting was scribed at the bottom - it read WEREWOMAN.

Meera could probably spend hours appraising that one composition. She was particularly struck by the smile of the woman in golden sunlight. It was not a smile of superiority or the inevitable happiness of seeing someone else in misery - it was a consummate smile that said: 'Whoever gets to this paradise comes by choice and effort and not luck. So the people stuck outside in the mire of their own choices should not blame their miseries on fate'. She found the thought so close to her heart and comforting that she made a mental note to ask the cafe owner more about the painting's details later on.

****

'Isn't it, Meera?' Ameya was enquiring something of her that she had missed in her pre-occupation with the painting.

'Sorry, I was looking at that painting, did not hear you. What were you saying?'

Everyone turned to look at the painting. Snigdha's husband exclaimed, 'Oh, that's really beautiful!'

'Kapil, Meera is herself a pretty good artist. I have seen some of her paintings. You should do an exhibition, M,' Ameya said. Then, deliberating over his own suggestion, he thoughtfully nodded and kept down his fork and knife to add, 'Yes, you should totally do an exhibition. In fact, they hold exhibitions right here! You should talk to the owner.'

Kapil also joined the discussion enthusiastically, 'Really? That's pretty cool. I will help promoting your stuff just so that I can boast that I know a famous artist.'

The guys laughed while Snigdha and Trapti forced a smile on their lips.

'Thanks, you guys are too polite. Anyway, I haven't painted in a while. So, I'm sorry Kapil, you will have to be content with having a 'struggling' artist as your friend,' Meera answered with a smile.

'Well, there are millions of struggling artists out there, no fun in that you know,' Snigdha rejoined. Upon realising everyone was flabbergasted, she added with a fake smile, 'So we would really hope that you become a renowned one.'

'I'm sure you do,' Meera said with no smile this time.

Luckily, the rest of the lunch was finished without further awkwardness and everyone got up to leave. Everyone shook hands, hugged as appropriate and as desired.

Vinay took Meera to a corner and apologised, 'I'm sorry I didn't listen to you. I don't think this was such a good idea after all.'

Meera nodded but added, 'It's actually my problem. I need to be prepared now for such exchanges, it's going to be a part of my life.'

He winced visibly at her uncensored admission.

She consoled him with little success and took his leave, heading to the loo to check her eyes. Her social skills and tolerance had all been tested today and she was glad it was over. It's funny how people change over time so that the whole dynamics of relationships alter, especially when you have lived apart for a significant time. She could barely feel any kinship to her so-called classmates today except Vinay and Ameya. Even if it wasn't for her extreme circumstances, she wondered if any friendship was possible with these people who could seem more agreeable only if treated exclusively as interesting strangers.

She was about to enter the washroom when she heard Trapti's voice inside saying something to the effect of,

'You watch out babes, your hubby was looking a lot in her direction.'

'For God's sake!' exclaimed the other voice and it wasn't hard to identify Snigdha.

Trapti was laughing, 'Okay, okay, maybe not a lot but still enough to make me warn you. You shouldn't underestimate our Miss Congeniality especially now when she is probably hunting for divorced guys.'

Meera felt herself melting down in a flame of shame and failure. She retreated before she could allow herself to even consider the route of confrontation. That a person should be able to fling such accusations at her was a thought provocative enough to consider self-annihilation.

She shut her eyes tight to engulf any tears that were trying to come out. The tumult of her feelings was beyond her capacity to control. All she could do was grab her car keys and rush out like a person on some mission. Ironically, it was exactly the opposite. She revved up the engine and took off down the road with a screeching sound. Fifteen minutes later, when she found herself on the highway did she realise that she had long lost any road or any purpose. She pulled the car over on the side, turned up the volume of the radio and burst into tears. That confined space which isolated her from anyone's eyes or ears felt like home so much so that she did not even try to suppress her cries. When she had cried her heart out, she started driving back.

Moments later, it had begun pouring. Except that the universe had decided to trifle with her, she could find no explanation of such voluminous rains on a December afternoon. She loved rains and if this was nature's way of consoling her after inflicting a miserable day, it seemed to have been done in an extremely bad taste. Rain, however, did lift her spirits to the extent possible under the circumstances. She was now in the city and while waiting on a traffic signal, she saw the board of 'crossword' and 'coffee junction' in the opposite pavement. It was not a hard decision to make.

****

After normalising herself with some reading exercises, she headed back home. As soon as she entered, her mother came forward to inform they were going to Mathura Vrindavan on a trip with her *Maasi's* family.

'I'm sorry I said yes without discussing with you. You would come *na*, darling?'

Meera felt scared at the prospect of a group trip but the childhood memories with her cousins comforted her.

'You should come, Meera, I think it will make us all happy,' her Dad said.

Meera nodded, 'Yes Ma, I'll come' and kissed her mother on her cheek.

PART TWO

Chapter NINE
Calling of Vrij

Who would have thought a journey could change one's destination? Meera did not consider herself religious and could never find herself harmonious with performing rites and rituals. But she felt close to Krsna and was curious to visit his birthplace, his childhood playground and see what had become of it.

Besides, she was a photographer at heart - every scene was meant for a frame and some frames became invaluable over time. The love for photography also developed a constant wanderlust in her. Every journey showed her some colors of life she had not seen before and that alone was a sufficient motive to travel. If nothing else, she could get good fodder for her camera.

It was a little chilly in the afternoon when Meera and her family arrived at Mathura railway station. She was traveling with her parents, aunt and two cousins with whom she had felt extremely close since childhood - younger Kavita and older Rohan.

What can one say about railways stations? And that too the Indian ones? These harbors of persistent and constant commuting are a true reflection of any country's populace and so it shouldn't be surprising to find chaos, crowd, poverty and resilience well and truly alive in here. The bickering and haggling between *coolies* and travelers might make a first world citizen stare in shock but when such a service is available in abundant supply, who will pay two hundred bucks to carry 5-6 suitcases across three platforms? For fifty rupees or so, one can find many willing porters putting unspeakable weights of luggage on their head and lanky shoulders and run up and down the stairs. If one were to give Olympic medals based on weight-one-can-carry to body-mass ratio, these coolies could probably beat professional weight lifting athletes. When a hungry stomach growls, a body develops the stamina without gym and protein shakes. When one is eating only one meal a day, it's not a matter of shame to sleep on the station floor with no *chaadar*. When one is barely making ends meet, hygiene or its lack thereby becomes a non-issue.

The air was filled with the smell of rodents, tea, sweat, piss and shit. The upper classes grimaced and covered their noses, the common man walked off. Indian railways carry a record 25 million passengers every day. When a train stops at a platform, the class distinction in Indian society manifests itself in the descending and ascending lot of passengers. Couple of elites from first AC, a handful of middle classes from second and third AC coaches, a multitude of lower classes from sleeper and general coaches - the constitution displays the fragmented Indian society in its crude reality.

****

After a painful journey in a local taxi that wobbled on the bumpy road from Mathura to Vrindavan, the party finally checked in to the lodge where they had luckily found a reservation at the last minute. Some auspicious Hindu month was going on and Vrindavan was swarming with visitors.

Meera quickly walked up to her room and thanked the Lord upon finding a clean bathroom where she relieved herself without any further delay - it had been a long time since she had used a facility, and the rattling ride from Mathura had only added to the misery. By balancing her fluid intakes, she had developed good stamina to withhold nature calls for longer durations and she knew it was going to prove pretty handy in India. Her biggest phobia and the one that had worsened by living in US was that of unclean toilets. Nothing scared her more than having to travel in India with no proper rest areas. A train journey was her worst nightmare not because of insecurity, but because of the ghastly toilets - you never knew what you were going to witness in there.

Vrindavan and a couple of towns around it collectively constitute the area known as *Vrij Mandal*. This is the land where Krsna spent his childhood. What caught Meera by surprise was discovering the fact that he was hardly ten or eleven years of age when he had left for Mathura. So all the superhuman tales we hear of him - lifting Govardhan, killing demons and many more - were performed by a child younger than ten years of age. One might still buy those but when it comes to the tales of *raas*, a human mind is sure to be stumped - how can one revere an amorous dance between a child and possibly an older girl? And between that child and hundred other women - not just women, married women? This is God we are talking about, so people are often ready to make exceptions but Meera did not accept it on face value. There had to be some deeper explanation behind it and it only added to her intrigue about Krsna.

One thing that immediately strikes you about the Mathura Vrindavan area is the number of foreign travelers. Over the years, Iskcon and other ashrams in Vrindavan have attracted a non-trivial following from the West. Clad in lose kurtis, skirts and dhotis, the fair skinned devotees and tourists have traveled thousands of miles to discover the ancient wisdom of our Vedas in a quest to lead a fulfilling and enlightened life. They roamed around the cramped *kunj* streets with one hand carrying the unpretentious rosary hidden in a *jap mala* bag - their hands mechanically counting the beads as they chant the mantra silently.

The most common means of conveyance is the cycle rickshaw that doesn't have a horn, instead the driver just shouts *'raadhe raadhe'* to get people to move out. Another vehicle one might spot on the broader lanes is the tempo - an open vehicle between the size of an auto and a SUV - with infinite capacity. Yes, don't be surprised to see literally 30-40 passengers riding on it together.

The streets are always buzzing with cows who are well fed by the devotees in remembrance of Krsna's avatar as a cow herder, and the roofs and electric poles are lined with bunches of red faced monkeys who feed themselves without your permission. They also claim books, spectacles and any small loose items in tourists' hands with alarming snap and sleight. One cannot experience Vrindavan without having been freaked out by their screeches, chatters and aerial dives between the roofs across the streets.

Chapter TEN
Three: Conversation of Hope

That evening after everyone had showered and rested a bit, the group was off to the Iskcon temple next door. Often denoted as the *videshi mandir*[20] by Indian devotees, Iskcon holds lesser religious significance for hard core Hindus but no one can deny its beauty and aesthetic.

The Hare Krsna *bhajan* was melodiously floating in the air as Meera entered the main checkered marble courtyard. She was not new to the chants as she had heard them many a time in Washington Square Park in Manhattan. What had made them more famous in United States was Steve Job's mentioning of the Hare Krsna temple in his iconic commencement speech at Stanford. This *bhajan* is unlike what one would traditionally hear at temples. It contains only two lines -

Hare Rama, Hare Rama, Rama Rama Hare Hare
Hare Krsna, Hare Krsna, Krsna Krsna Hare Hare

It starts off in a gentle tempo by a lead singer at the microphone supported by a couple of musicians playing harmonium, *kartal* and *dholak*. The devotees inevitably join in on the chorus. The same lines are repeated again and again in a gradually ascending tempo. Again and again. The words are now being sung faster, the *dholak* is being beaten with quicker hands, the harmonium's keys are being punched in an accelerated rhythm and the wrists of the *kartal* player are being flicked at a brisker pace. The devotees are in a trance with their eyes closed and heads shaking to the tune. Their voices have unconsciously elevated in an effort to reach God himself. The tempo eventually reaches its pinnacle in amplitude and speed. At

---

[20] foreigners' temple

this moment the instruments are paused and the lead *kirtan* singer reconnects to the slower tempo with something similar to an *alaap*.

This cycle of five to six minutes is continuously repeated in the evening *kirtans*. Its redundancy has yet to affect its charm as the size of the evening congregation has only been growing. Half of the population at Iskcon is foreign adding to its western image - devotees from Americas, Europe, Australia and every corner, with the possible exception of Africa, flock here.

As the sun sets and darker skies emerge, *deepdaan* services begin where in Iskcon volunteers hand out small pre-lit earthen lamps to every visitor in the temple courtyard. These lamps are fitted with a thick cotton wick soaked in wax that remains lit up to six minutes which is sufficient time to visit the idols and do *aarti*, and are duly collected back in a waste bin. This illuminates the temple dimly and serenely with bare minimum electricity.

As Meera held the tiny *diya*, inhaled the smell of pious fire and felt the *bhajan* verses sinking in from her ears to her soul, she was scintillated. This sensation was new to her and she let herself absorb it fully. She moved along the queue and stood riveted in front of the handsome idols of Krsna and Radha. There is something divine about the work of the Iskcon designers which reflects itself in the idols, drawings, paintings and every aspect of the temple's visual elements. The figures and expressions of the deities are drawn with such mystical genius that an onlooker can't look away easily.

The painting of Yasoda scolding a mischievous Krsna will bring an inevitable smile to your lips. A bystander might not even be taken aback if the *bal* Krsna succeeds in wringing his wrists out of his furious mother's hold and jumps out of the frame to abscond to a safer place. The picture of a humbled Arjun looking up to Krsna, who at his wish is displaying his magnificent *viraat swaroop* will make one irrevocably bow his head and wonder, if just for a moment, at the insignificance of his desires before this Supreme Lord.

Having carefully toured the temple premises, Meera took a seat in front of the *kirtan mandli* and joined in on the chanting.

Some time had passed and she was thoroughly soaked in the spirit of Krsna when her eyes met those of the man who was playing the harmonium. He had quickly averted his gaze before she could look away. She tried not giving undue importance to the event and continued to chant calmly. But forcing not to look in that direction again was nothing but an acknowledgement in itself. So she tried freeing herself of that enforcement by letting her eyes wander freely, but it wasn't to be. Now, when her eyes went back to that person, they lingered for a while noticing his appearance and adroitness with the harmonium. He was a fair young guy with short clipped hair and oval face. A saffron *teeka* adorning his forehead and a *rudraksha maala* around his neck reaffirmed his religious inclinations. He was wearing a loose fitting *khaadi kurta*, white pajama and the look of an artist deeply absorbed in his performance, contrary to the distracted countenance she had witnessed few minutes ago.

She let her gaze follow and then rest at his fingers that were deftly dancing on the harmonium keys. She did not realise when her lips curved into a smile. Her mind had traveled from the skillful fingers to the vision of a graceful young Krsna mounting the hoods of Kalia, the serpentine demon, who is now about to begin dancing amidst the tormented waves of Yamuna. The enthrallment of seeing the originator of all art forms wielding his performance at a stage as suitably unique and unstable as that of the gilded, heaving and thorny heads of a tortured serpent was enough for her to lose any sense of time or place. The energetic waves in the Yamuna nearly hypnotised her and brought back the memory of the high tide of Hudson that had nearly engulfed her. As she looked up, she saw Krsna's feet jumping and moving flawlessly on the shifting hoods while his lips held on to a smooth rhythm on the flute. Did she see him smiling and opening his eyes briefly? She felt an excitement akin to the one she had felt when she had turned to find her savior that night and had seen no one.

Long minutes must have passed by as she experienced the performance most extraordinary in her gifted imagination, vision or whatever one can call it. When she finally looked up, her eyes met those of the same guy again but this time, he did not look away. Her neck jolted sideways. She consciously kept sitting for a few more minutes before getting up and walking to the back of the courtyard behind the platform where the *kirtan* was going on. Feeling free of a watchful eye, she looked back at the podium and was surprised to find a stranger sitting at the harmonium. Her disappointment had barely taken its place on her physiognomy when she saw the familiar person walking towards her.

****

'*Hare* Krsna,' he said with a slight bow.

'Oh! *Hare* Krsna,' she said joining her palms in *namaskar* gesture in response.

'You were smiling as if you had seen something.'

'I thought that would be a pretty common sight here. Aren't people supposed to see *something* here that makes them smile?'

The man smiled.

'I am Madhur, I belong to the Iskcon committee that oversees this temple.'

'Oh okay. Hi. I mean *namaste*. Sorry, but I'm not into joining religious committees.'

Madhur touched the *teeka* on his forehead and then the beads around his neck. 'I see, did I scare you so?'

'No, not until you introduced yourself.'

'Pardon my appearance, we are not a cult or anything. We definitely do not force members into it,' he added with a purposeful frivolity. 'I just happened to notice you back there and felt like knowing you more.'

'In my experience, that's a good line of action for recruiting someone into your community. That's how it usually begins and then ends with *why don't you read some of our philosophy?'* she said with a wry smile.

He grinned and shook his head as if surrendering to the accusation so acutely drawn that there was no scope for proving one's innocence.

'But I can still claim that you are more spiritual than most of the people here. And I wouldn't want to harass you.' He took a respectful bow and started to leave.

'I am spiritual and I think the same of you. I'm sorry if I distracted you while you were playing in the *kirtan*.'

She had carefully uttered those words and knew the effect they would produce. Madhur had deserted any thoughts of leaving.

'I can't lie in a temple and I do not lie anyway. You did distract me.'

'I am sorry for that although I can't claim to know the reason.'

'You looked too sincere for your age.'

'So do you.'

'It took me years to get here. And that's why I took the liberty of assuming that you belonged to some organisation too.'

'Life teaches what no organisation can.'

'So, would you mind telling me why you were smiling?'

'Not in the least. Your fingers on the keyboard reminded me of Krsna dancing on Kalia,' her eyes looked steadily into those of Madhur as she spoke the unlikely words in a manner incongruously casual. She noticed the expressions of her interlocutor taking on the gravity now demanded by her confession.

She continued, 'I witnessed the long dance - the lotus feet rhythmically jumping from one hood to another till the demon succumbed.' She continued looking steadily at him in a manner that challenged - *let's see if you have the courage to believe that.*

'I wish I had your eyes,' came the solemn reply.

Whatever Meera had expected, it was not such a humble acceptance. Her face softened as if she did not feel a need of guarding herself against him anymore.

'Thanks for believing my words.'

'I would have known if you tried to lie. So, thanks for telling the truth. God, why didn't I try to get into this so-called *life school*? My time would have been better spent,' he said humorously.

'Don't be so sure. It is the most expensive school, takes a lot from you,' her voice trailed off.

He watched her closely and saw the transformation in her eyes. 'I will only say this and I hope you will trust me. Whatever you have paid has been worth what you have become now. May Krsna bless you.'

Before she had a chance to respond, her cousins had come in search of her. 'There you are! We had been looking for you everywhere.'

With a rushed goodbye, she took his leave.

That night in her bed, Meera reflected on the day's events and thought she had already got more in the first day of the trip than what she could have bargained for. Vrindavan was acting as a powerful catalyst to her capabilities of experiencing Krsna. That did not surprise her. After all, this was Krsna's territory. Every person, every cow, every beast and every vegetation breathed and lived him, they existed just for him. One could not walk ten steps without hearing 'raadhe raadhe'. So, why shouldn't her purported connection to Krsna find itself empowered here?

Chapter ELEVEN
Atonement

In America, people talk about the weather a lot, work, food, dating, workout and travel. In India, topics are confined to family, religion and jobs. Travel for pleasure's sake is catching on among working youths these days, but family trips mostly remain religion oriented. Adventure as a travel category never made much sense to Indian parents. Meera did not talk about her bungee jump at home else she might have heard something to the effect of, '*Yahi bacha tha, bachche ab pahaadon se kood rahe hain*[21]*!*'

C'est la vie.

****

Alarms and phones went off with different tunes at five a.m. Following few snoozes and wake up calls, the family had gotten ready for an ambitious itinerary for the day. It was a day to conquer the famous Govardhan - a hill considered to be a natural form of Krsna himself. Although the hill is no longer visible now, the popular custom is to circumambulate it so as to heighten one's devotion and consciousness.

As it happens, popular lore from mythology is quickly adapted by masses in India and Govardhan *parikrama* is daily performed by thousands of devotees on bare foot. Many people know the story behind Govardhan and how Krsna lifted it to shelter *brijwasis* from the wrath of Indra. But the lesser known fact is how it marks a pivotal milestone in the history of Hinduism. While asking the *brijwasis* to offer prayers to forces of nature instead of trying to please demigods, Krsna preached an ideology

---

[21] kids are now jumping off mountains!

radically different from the one preceding it. This also marks the event when he professed the *karma yoga*[22] for the first time; the philosophy which would very soon become the crux of Bhagvad Gita and an eternal lighthouse, the only source of light for the lost mankind. This is why he appears as the most influential and reformative among the deities.

'How long is it, Uncle?' enquired an ever curious Kavita to which Sumer replied, 'It's around twenty one kilometers *bete*.'

Her eyebrows inched up, 'So how long will it take?'

'Might take us eight-nine hours.'

She reflected upon that quietly. She clearly had never walked even half of this distance. For that matter, none of them had except for Sumer.

Tactics were decided and supplies packed. As soon as anyone felt they couldn't go any longer, a rickshaw would be hired. No one dared to go shoeless. 'I would rather hope to complete it wearing my shoes than trying bare foot and failing midway,' was the mutual consensus.

Rohan whispered to Meera who had mostly been silent on the whole issue, 'Are you conserving energy, sister? Good idea because I can't bet against you fainting on the road.'

'Shut up! We'll see who starts making excuses midway,' came the answer with a punch on Rohan's rotund belly.

'Ow! Yeah I, at least, won't die of malnourishment. Anyway, why are we fighting? We know who's going to be the first to hop on a rickshaw.'

Both started looking at the plump Kavita who was finishing her *aloo paratha* sincerely and broke into laughter.

An hour later after paying respect at Giriraj temple that was erected at the starting point of the *parikrama*, the group started

---

[22] discipline of action

their journey. It was not hard to miss the starting point as people suddenly fell to their knees at this point and bowed down their head on a damar road. The devotees who vow to do the *dandvat parikrama*[23] begin prostrating right here. Meera's family found itself in a minority who were wearing sandals.

****

The rest of the group had taken a rickshaw after three hours of walking but Meera, Sumer and Rohan had persisted on foot. With juice and tea breaks, some heart-to-heart about the old days and Sumer's religious anecdotes, they kept walking.

Sumer shared a story, 'Once, Swami Tulsidas visited a Krsna temple in Vrij and was mesmerised by the beauty of the idol. But being a follower of Ram who is identified by his image of carrying a bow and arrow, Tulsidas ji said before praying-

Kaah kahaun chhabi aajuki, bhale bane ho naath

Tulsi mastak tab navai, jab dharo dhanush shar haath

That means - O Lord, how shall I describe your splendor today, for you look enchanting. Tulsidas will, however, bow down his head only when you take the bow and the arrow in your hands.'

'Then?' asked Rohan impatiently on Sumer's pause.

'What can happen then? Hail the power of such a devotee - it is said that when Tulsidas looked again, there was the transformed idol indeed with bow and arrow in hands. Do you know what he said next?'

Meera and Rohan both shook their heads.

'He said -

Kit murali kit chandrika, kit gopin ka saath

Tulsi Das ke karane Nath bhaye Raghu Nath

---

[23] Variation of the circumspect journey where a person lies prostrating at each step.

Where did the flute go, the crown and the *gopis*? It is for Tulsi's sake that Krsna has transformed into Ram.'

****

Eerie monkeys snatching off bags of chips from their hands and the deserted ruins of ancient temples kept the fourteen mile walk eventful and interesting.

The last mile was the hardest as the feet and calves had become numb except for tiny specks that could still absorb the sensation of pain. As they walked on the needles of uneven concrete, the pain shot to unbearable heights and their faces convulsed in agony. After seven hours, the three of them were bowing their heads down on the end point of the *parikrama*.

Everyone was hungry, yet too tired to eat. Each passing minute was making them aware of a new muscle in their body just by its capacity to ache. Finishing a simple dinner in the cafeteria of their lodge, everyone retired early to the beds. Except Meera who requested to catch the last *kirtan* at Iskcon temple next door.

****

Meera entered the Iskcon premises limping and managed her way to where the *kirtan* was going on. She looked searchingly for a couple of minutes before finally spotting Madhur at the *deepdaan* service. She went and took one lamp from him. He smiled at her and said, '*Hare* Krsna.'

'*Hare* Krsna,' she gently bowed.

She completed her round and came to sit in the middle of the courtyard where Madhur could see her. After seeing her glance at him a couple of times, Madhur handed his duty over to a friend and came to join Meera.

'How was your day?'

'Good, I just got back from the Govardhan *parikrama*.'

'Great, how did you like it? Seen him holding the Govardhan?'

'No, I made sure I wouldn't.'

'Why would you do that?'

'To see if I still see him.'

'And did you?'

'No.'

'You seem disappointed. How did you make sure, by the way?'

'I did not let myself stand at a place for enough time to...to let him appear.'

'Hmmm....How did you find the *parikrama*? I didn't think it would interest you.'

'Why not?'

'It is supposedly an orthodox practice to please God, doesn't appeal that much to the younger generations.'

'Hmm.'

'Oh, you didn't tell me your name. I realised it after you had gone yesterday.'

'Yeah, had to go suddenly, sorry about that. My name is Meera.'

Madhur smiled and asked, 'Seriously?'

'What?'

'You are Meera?'

'Why can't I be?'

'Wow, you always talk in negatives, don't you?'

'I'm sorry, I'm just a bit rattled. Yes, my name is Meera...what's wrong with it?'

'Nothing, I just meant I should have guessed it. Who can see

Krsna? Of course, Meera. I guess if I really wanted to see God, my parents should have named me Surdas. Sorry that sounded wrong, by see I mean experience. By the way, it's said he could actually talk to Krsna. Sorry for my ramblings, never mind.'

Meera looked ahead abstractly, 'No, I know what you mean. You know I didn't do the *parikrama* to please God or to build some good will...*punya* and all.'

'Don't tell me you wanted to do some physical exercise because you could find cleaner marathon tracks for that.'

She looked at him to acknowledge his attempts at humour and then again turned her eyes to some point of interest at infinity. 'I needed to pay for a few things I am not proud of.'

Madhur nodded in an impressed manner.

'You continue to amaze me. I have seen many people here, they come for different rhymes and reasons. Youths come for tourism, jobs, love affairs, family affairs. Elders come for salvation and family welfare. Famous people come for more fame. Rich people come for more money. Poor people come for livelihood and miracles. Very few people come for atonement. I can't imagine what sins you might have committed and I hope now that you have done something - I would say a pretty significant thing - to atone for those, you are feeling better.'

Meera nodded gently and continued to look afar. A few moments passed as both of them sat silently - Meera out of a need to feel and rest (after all she hadn't still regained consciousness in her left calf) and Madhur out of understanding. He hadn't gotten much time to *know* her but he had noticed she was different, less talkative, less inquisitive and a bit lost. He felt she needed a good listener and someone who could communicate at her level, so he was content in aiding rather than initiating conversations.

'You think I'm...weird or loose in my head, don't you?'

'Well, you are wired differently I must say and I mean it in a positive way before you jump to conclusions. Why bother though?

Everyone is different in their own ways....some deny it, some face it. As far as being weird is concerned, you are not insane if that is what you meant. You are looking for something, some understanding and perhaps you feel that people don't understand you.'

She was now staring at him and was about to say something when she stopped herself. 'I'm really concerned now.'

'About what?'

'That I might end up joining your cult. They seem to be teaching some effective psychology to you guys.'

He chuckled, 'That is a big compliment.'

'Jokes apart, yes, you do touch some nerve in me that makes me respond. I've never been a great conversationalist and talking to people tires me because almost no one understands you and I don't enjoy making small talk that much. But you make me talk somehow...I like talking to you.'

'Well, I'm glad if I can help.' At that note, he took out a scribbling pad and pen from his pocket. He wrote something on a piece of paper and handed it to her. 'That's my contact information. Just in case you want to talk ever when I am not physically around. And that is usually given only when you join the cult but I have made an exception for you.' Both of them smiled.

She watched him go and join the *kirtan*. 'How old must he be?' she thought. Not more than thirty and he looked scholarly. In fact, many of the Iskcon volunteers that she had seen in the temple looked young, energetic, well read and intelligent.

Did she really believe in Iskcon or any such organisation that professed to be an authority on religion or God? She did believe in the power of an effective teacher though and sometimes, you do need a guide. There was no denying that she was restless.

Did she really see Krsna or was he a figment of her imagination? What was she supposed to do with a gifted vision if that is what it was? She had tried life as a normal human being does - she loved, she consumed, she thought her life was simple and not sinful, she thought she was 'good enough' but life had turned upside down.

What could she possibly have done to deserve such harsh treatment from life?

Is that why she had started to think more about God these days?

Was she trying to please him now that no other resort existed? Is that good or bad?

Thus went on her *antar-dvand*[24] as she contemplated her next steps. She felt she was being given a chance to find the answers. Decisively, she got up and went up to the place where the chants were going on. With some difficulty, she hustled her way to a pillar close to the lead singer and leaned on it patiently. She waited.

The crowd started thinning. Nearly half an hour later, the chants stopped and it was time to close down the temple for the day. Meera waited till a relative quiet had established.

'I want to learn how I can find God,' she said in a clear and slightly raised voice that made everyone look at her, including Madhur whose intrigued countenance made it clear that he was expecting neither her presence nor her question. A faint smile had emerged on many faces but no one had ventured to speak anything.

Madhur finally stepped forward and said, 'Why don't you join us for the session tomorrow morning? Dr. Naren is giving a discourse here.'

'Will that help me find God?'

'Yes, but you need to bring your *nishtha* along.'

'Ok, I will.' She nodded and bowed slightly to take her leave.

Madhur reciprocated with the gesture and words, '*Hare* Krsna.'

---

[24] Inner debate

The bizarre incident kept replaying in Meera's mind as she tried to sleep at night. The rest of her family had retired directly after dinner and everyone was asleep when she came back from Iskcon. Her legs were still hurting when she moved, so she tried to lie still. She was excited and curious for the next day, she did not know what to expect. What had Madhur exactly meant by bring your *nishtha* along? *Nishtha* is faith; did he doubt her faith? She did have faith, didn't she?

She kept pursuing these thoughts late into the night. In the wake of her extreme tiredness and anxiety, sleep had refused to come for a long time. It wasn't before three in the morning that her sleep finally claimed its ground.

Chapter TWELVE
Divine Teacher

The big space in front of the main idols was packed with the audience waiting for Dr. Naren. He was a renowned scholar on religions and taught a course named 'Global Reach of Religions' at Georgia Tech University. Meera had come on time and taken a seat in the middle. Everyone applauded as Dr. Naren made his entrance.

Madhur waved to Meera and invited her to join the Iskcon committee members in front. She hesitatingly obeyed and went on to sit next to him. Dr. Naren had occupied his seat in the front of a chamber that contained the life-size statue of Bhaktivedanta Swami Prabhupada, the founder-*acharya* of Iskcon.

He began the lecture with a story of his meeting with Swami Prabhupada and how he had helped shape his earlier beliefs.

'I was an inquisitive person as I am sure a lot of you are. Swami (Prabhupad) answered all of my queries with a humble smile. This was very different from the reactions I was used to getting. My family had relocated to Canada a generation ago but they could never let go of their faith and religious inclinations. To ensure that I didn't turn out a pagan, they constantly held *poojas*, *yagya* and *pravachan* meetings at our home when I was a child. It got me curious alright, but most of the priests who I talked to took offense on being questioned by a teenager. Thankfully, that did not thwart the L'Enfant terrible in me.'

The pin drop silence in the audience was broken by chuckles.

'And during one of these quests, I came across Swami ji in 1970 at a University in Canada; he had successfully established the Krsna consciousness movement in the West by then. I did not expect much when I began but I was a less terrible child by the time he was done answering me. And he did answer me. That is one of the traits of a master - he can quench the thirst of knowledge. In fact, only he can. Once I had those answers, and I'm not saying that I developed a halo or became the omniscient sage, I felt my journey had started. Another thing that impressed me about the incident was that Swami ji did not force me to become what he wanted but he guided me on how I can pursue my objectives in a more spiritual manner.

After that, I met him again twice on different occasions. When he learned of my desire to become a teacher, he held my hand and said, "It is not easy to be a guru and you have to show them the light. But in this process, you will assimilate their sins and suffer for them, you will have to. You will lose your perfection in the process and you will strive to get it back, so remember that a guru needs to work harder than a pupil." It hit my brain hard when I heard the process being described in those terms. I am sure I did not even comprehend it fully but the event made it clear to me that I should serve as a teacher. At that time, I couldn't understand what sufferings are entailed in teaching a normal course at a school. He was talking of the suffering that a spiritual master bears for his disciples because disciples come with their sins and a spiritual master has to take responsibility for those in a way. Being a spiritual master was nowhere in my career plans. So, I could not have possibly known that I would act as a spiritual preacher some day. But he already knew that I would and that's what he was referring to.'

The silence in the audience became more silent if that is possible. Meera was listening carefully and was completely absorbed. She didn't know what to expect but the sermon sounded promising. Often, religious sermons tend to jump into mythological realms without constructing a proper bridge from the real world.

Saints breaking into dances on stage was beyond her comprehension especially when same speaker was seen spouting nonsensical political statements afterwards. She was shocked to hear a famous spiritual leader saying *"Sita lakshaman rekha paar karengi, to haran to hoga hi*[25]*"* on the matter of a rape case. Another so-called guru had said, "The girl should have begged the assaulters and made them her brothers to prevent the rape".

How such views reconciled with spiritual awareness was too baffling for her common senses. So, a talk such as this was a welcome sound to her ears and a mind that was starving for some food for thought.

Dr. Naren continued with the current standing of religion in his opinion and discussed various occult practices he had seen in different corners of the world. 'I understand that calling yourself an atheist is in vogue these days. It appeals to the younger generation not having to believe in anything but themselves. But I ask them why they still feel depressed and helpless then. And more importantly, what do you do when you feel that way? Does your self-belief rescue you on its own or do you go to the closest bar and get drunk? By the way, any guesses on where the closest bar is? It is the refrigerator.'

Laughter broke out. Meera was grinning, thinking of her previous colleagues and friends who exchanged their failures or depressions for hangovers.

'The so called atheists follow another religion that they are not aware of. It is called alcoholism.'

The lecture ended with loud applause. The audience started dispersing and a few devotees made their way to the front to chat further with Dr. Naren. Meera waited for her turn that came in twenty minutes. She gently moved to the front and introduced herself, 'That was a very inspiring talk Professor. My name is Meera. I'm not an Iskcon member or anything but I'm seeking God. Can you...help me?'

Dr. Naren chortled. 'Yes, I can help you. Even these people can help you,' he said pointing to Madhur and other members.

---

[25] If Sita crosses her limits, then she is responsible for her abduction.

'I want to reach God. I think...I know he is there but I don't know how to experience him fully.'

'That's a start. There are ways to reach him. In Gita, Krsna has talked of three ways to do that - knowledge, action and devotion. Do you know which one is the best?'

Meera shook her head in negation.

'Contrary to how people interpret that Gita is more about action alone, I feel Krsna said all paths, all yogas, are equally effective. You choose what works for you. It is said, *bhakti* or pure devotion is easier to follow. If you surrender your senses and awareness to him, then he takes you into his custody. You become his responsibility now. Let him control you. So, while you just wanted to reach him, now you have liberation.'

'How do I get *bhakti*? How do I know if I have *nishtha* or not?'

'If you didn't, you wouldn't be asking all these questions.'

Meera had knelt down and her inner turmoil had started surfacing. Her eyes were now wearing the pain she kept suppressed in public. With a hoarse voice, she asked, 'I have had some troubles in life...some big troubles. I see darkness ahead and only thing that has kept me sane is relating myself to Krsna. I want to be happy but I don't know if that can ever happen again. Will I ever be happy again? I don't know. I want my life to get back to normal, I want it to be fine.'

Dr. Naren smiled. 'Let me tell you a story. There was a blind widow in a village. She was very poor and had a tough life. Her sole support was her son whom she doted on. Needless to say, he was her everything. One day he died in his sleep. The old woman tried waking him up but obviously he didn't move. She got very worried, so she called upon her neighbors and asked them to wake him up. Her neighbors soon realised that the boy was already dead but they thought if they told that to her, she wouldn't be able to bear the shock and might die. So they just said that he was in a very deep sleep and that they couldn't get him to wake up. Now, there was a learned *sadhu* who used to live in a temple nearby. They told her that he might be able to wake him up. She agreed to go to him. They helped carry the body of her son and took her to the temple and told the full story to the *sadhu*. Thereupon, the woman asked the sadhu to get his son back up. The *sanyasi* said, "*Amma*, I will wake him up but I need you to bring me five mustard seeds from a house in the village where no one has died. Remember, we cannot wake him up without those mustard seeds. And you should get them from any house where no one has died." The old woman agreed and set upon her task. She went to the first house on her way back and asked if anyone had ever died in there. "Yes, my grandmother died here last year." She moved on. "Yes, we just had the funeral of my brother last month" was the next and so on. Everywhere, she got the same reply with tears - sometime it was mother, brother, grandfather. She had checked out all the houses by now and disheartened, she returned. She poured out the story to the sadhu who made her sit and gave her water. Then he gently told her, "Do you see Amma? There is no one who has not felt the pain of death in his or her family. It has happened to me and everyone. It is how God made us. Your son has also died but why do you worry? We are all here to die one day, so why not devote our life to a Godly life? You make me your son and you shall be my mother from today. Whatever *rookha sookha* I eat, I will first offer it to you." When the news was put in such a perspective to her, the woman was able to accept it peacefully. So my dear Meera, we have all been in pain. It is one of the stops on the bus of life. You can choose to get down there or you can ride on.'

Seeing a smile blossom on Meera's face, he continued, 'What's that *bhajan*, Madhur? *Kaun kehte hain Bhagwan sunte nahi?*'

Everyone looked expectantly at Madhur who was also smiling now. He said, 'Yes, it's the *Achyutam Keshavam* bhajan. It says - *Kaun kehte hain Bhagwan aate nahi? Tum Meera ke jaise bulaate nahi*[26].'

---

[26] Who says God doesn't come? You don't call him like Meera.

Dr. Naren first hummed the line that made everyone smile towards Meera and then he continued, 'You are Meera, my dear. If you can't find him, who can? Live up to your name.'

'Last question, Professor.' She looked around hesitatingly like a child forced to confess something embarrassing in front of his class. 'I see Krsna. That is I *think* I see Krsna and he once spoke to me too. I don't know how exactly it happens but I do see him at times. I see him as clearly as I'm seeing you right now but I may not be able to draw him for you, I can never define his face but I can see him... moving...dancing...' She paused but got no encouragement from the person in front.

Dr. Naren was still looking composedly at her. He finally broke his silence, 'When did you start seeing him?'

'Few months ago when I was in a lot of trouble, and restless. I used to meditate with his thought in my mind...and he began emerging in a...I don't know what to call it...in a more defined form in my vision.' She didn't know what response to expect but she hoped it wouldn't be an outright rejection.

'That must be a boon as well as a burden for you. You have to make yourself stronger.'

Meera's eyes had welled up. She was touched by the elegance and accuracy of his description, which was weird because even she had not realised that it was, in a way, a burden too.

'Read good positive thoughts, pray with a bare heart and find yourself. We will meet again and you will have more things to tell me by then. Take this time to make yourself stronger.' Thus speaking these final words, Dr Naren got up. He had a flight to catch, so the devotees scurried around to see to his last minute arrangements.

****

After Dr Naren's departure, Madhur approached Meera and offered her coffee at the temple cafeteria. She willingly agreed after realising that in her hurry to come on time that morning, she had not found time to have her regular tea or coffee - one thing that she rarely lived without. She sipped on her hot black coffee and watched Madhur drink his pinkish tea.

'What's that?' she curiously asked.

'It's Iskcon's trademark herbal tea. So, how did you find Dr. Naren? Did he help? Or did I waste your time?' he asked with a hint of smile that covered his anxiety.

'He was very different from anyone I have heard before. And seemed more authentic. I wish there was more time. I have lot of questions. Some are pretty stupid but still.'

'There are no stupid questions. At least, I can't imagine them in your head.'

'No, I do.'

'Give me an example.'

She chuckled, 'Okay, here's one. So, in Hinduism, you hear about good...or great...people getting liberated and other being reborn as something else...'

'Yeah, depending on their karma.'

'Right, karma. So, I could be born as an octopus or an ant could be born as a human. It all depends on what kind of lifestyle I led.'

'Um okay, that's simplifying it too much but let's see where you are going with this.'

'Yeah, I mean...so, anyone doing good is progressed upwards to better animals and any human doing good is liberated. Anyone doing bad is demoted. Right?'

He smiled, 'Right except that not just humans can be liberated. Remember the *vaanar sena* from Ramayan? They were liberated too.'

'Hm yeah. And where or how are new people getting in? I mean the population keeps growing, so there have to be new souls floating around, right? So, that's the first question. How does a new soul come into being...from scratch that is?'

'What do you mean?'

'And secondly, if all the time good people are being skimmed from the top, I mean, since they attain moksha and are not coming back, are you not removing good and adding more bad souls all the time? Then, how will the world ever get to be a better place?'

'Yeah but any soul can do good now. Anyway it's not that the soul is bad. It's the karma. The soul is neutral. So it's neutral souls turning good or bad.'

Meera thought over that and then nodded slowly, 'I guess you are right. A bad person could be a good cow reincarnated. Hmm yeah that makes sense.'

'Does it? Thank God I passed the exam else Iskcon would have kicked me out. By the way, say that again. Do you know how funny it sounds?'

Both of them laughed.

'Wait though. As per your logic, it might happen that all of the neutral souls become good and be liberated. That means the population reducing...but that never happens, you know.'

'Yeah because all of them don't do good. So the fact that the population keeps growing means that more animals are doing good than men doing bad and retrograding to animals. That is one possibility and secondly, more new souls are being introduced in *maanav yoni.*'

'So, that wasn't a stupid question after all,' Meera said with a satisfied look and smile. She continued, 'But the meeting ended so abruptly, I didn't know what Dr. Naren meant by saying that we'll meet again.'

'He rarely says things like that, so consider it special attention on his behalf. You can find out about his schedule and see if you can meet him next at some place convenient for you. He emphasised that you should build your inner strength.'

'Yeah, what do you think he meant by that?'

He kept his cup down and took a deliberate pause. 'I think he was hinting that these visions of yours might prove too much for a weaker mind. I have heard that people who develop occult powers can find it draining. Like a person I know who had *siddhi* in Goddess Kali. He had almost reduced to half and was mentally drained since developing this psychic sense. I am not sure if he meant that your visions are psychic but he seemed pretty clear on one thing - that you should strengthen your inner self so as to not be burned out by such a powerful experience. That's my two cents but don't take it on face value. I might be wrong. If I were in your place, I would consider myself fortunate and take it as a divine indication that you are special and you should not let the mundane problems of life shake you.'

Meera lowered her eyelids as the mention of her problems reminded her how she had revealed her weak emotions and possibly tears in front of Dr. Naren and Madhur. What must he be thinking? But she fought back against the subduing feelings and looked up, 'I didn't get a chance to thank you.'

He looked at her in a puzzled manner, 'What for?'

'One...for inviting me to this lecture.'

'It was a public event, I just happened to inform you.'

She nodded and got up. 'Also for being nice. And, for the coffee.' She started to leave, seeing which he got up as well.

He extended his hand, 'Take care and be happy.'

She shook his hand and smiled, 'You too.'

Chapter THIRTEEN
Devotion

'How many temples are here? We have seen so many and you keep telling me there are more,' a tired Kavita complained to her mother while slipping off her sandals at Baanke Bihari temple and standing in the long queue to get in. Meera and Rohan giggled.

Her mother hushed her up in anger, '*Aise nahi bolte.* This is THE temple to visit in Vrindavan. This is the *authentic* one. *Hai na Jija ji? Yahin Bhagwan ki moorti prakat hui thi na?*[27]'

Meera's father came to the rescue, 'Yes, Kavita. In fact, everyone should listen while we stand in the queue.' And, the lecture followed on how Baanke Bihari's idol revealed itself to Swami Haridas and hence, the historic importance.

Kavita's mother continued, '*Iskcon me kya hai? Kuch videshi aakar samajhte hain ki humse zyada bhakti unhe aati hai? Ek videshi ne Gita kya padh li, humse zyada gyaani ho gaye wo log?*[28]'

'Iskcon was not founded by a *Videshi*, Mom,' Rohan protested. 'He just helped spread the word to other cultures. Why are you bringing that in here? Shouldn't we be happy that even westerners are believing in our religion?'

'*Maante kya na karte? Unka religion to unhe kahin le ja nahi pa raha, to hamare paas hi to aayenge na*[29].'

Rohan bowed his head in a sarcastic *namaskar* to his mother to

---

[27] Isn't it brother-in-law? This is where the statue appeared miraculously, no?
[28] What's there in Iskcon? Those foreigners think they are more religious than us? One foreigner came and studied Gita and now they think they are more knowledgeable?
[29] What choice do they have? Their religion is getting them no where, so where else would they go?

indicate he had surrendered and had no intent of arguing further. Everyone laughed. They had now entered the main hall and the queue in front of them began winding like the anatomy of a maze. The Lord's idol was now visible at the far end of the hall and Meera looked up curiously to see the three bends that gave it its trademark name of 'Baanke'.

Her father's background commentary floated in her ears as she watched the big eyes, jet black form and ornate ensemble, 'Bihari ji, if you look closely, is in a united form of Krsna and Radha. You will see the idol adorning both male and female jewellery. Did you just notice the *purdah* that the priest put in front of the idol? They do that every few minutes.'

Kavita excitedly interjected, 'Why?'

'So that a devotee does not take the Lord with him.'

'What! How can one take him...he is so far in there?'

'Well *bete*, Bihari ji is said to be very attached to his devotees and its said *ki agar koi bhakt bahut leen ho kar unhe dekhta rahe, to Bhagwan uske saath chal dete hain*[30]. That's why the priest keeps bringing the *purdah* so that no one can look at him continuously.'

Meera was now looking at the idol steadily - not to test the story but because she felt irresistibly enamored by its beauty. It was very different from other illustrations of Krsna and from how he appeared in her visions. Soon they reached the front where she continued to watch him closely. She murmured, '*Mere saath chalo Bihari ji.*[31]' But nothing happened.

****

Lord Shiv wanted to see *raas* once and asked Krsna to invite him. But he told him that only *gopis* are permitted in the land of *raas*. So, Mahadev obligingly took the form of a *gopi* and visited *raas*

---

[30] If a devotee stares at the idol with pure devotion, then Lord Bihari goes off with him.
[31] Come with me Lord.

as Gopeshwar Mahadev. Such were the anecdotes that floated in and around Vrindavan.

Countless temples, countless stories but one bottomline - Divine identity of Radha Krsna still dominated Vrindavan and the nearby Vrij area. The world existed in just two words - Radha - one who seeks liberation - and Krsna - one who is all attractive. Magic happened on this land where the Lord had displayed his enchanting *leelas* to the dwellers.

Passing through alleys so narrow that no vehicle bigger than a cycle rickshaw could drive through them, Meera overheard a small kid asking his father, '*Papa, yahan Krsna ka season chal raha hai kya*[32]? His photos are around everywhere.' She could not help smiling.

Immersing in increasing awe for her Krsna, Meera found herself next in Nidhivan - the garden of *tulsi* where *raas* happened. *Raas* - the divine dance of Krsna and countless *gopis* - beyond the conception of mortals and their frames of mind. The guide disappointed her too by not being able to answer her queries.

Inside the Nidhivan was situated a temple where it was said that Radha Krsna prepare themselves for the *raas-raatri* every night.

'What? So *raas* happens here every night? Live? You mean Krsna ji visits this place every night, he will come tonight?' Rohan asked curiously.

The guide nodded and continued, 'The entry is closed after the night *aarti* and no one is allowed to stay afterwards. But in the past, some people tried to sneak in and tried to see the *raas* with their eyes. They did not survive the night and were found either dead or out of their senses to narrate whatever they had witnessed in the night. Either way, no one has been able to bring to public knowledge what happens in Nidhivan at night. *Jisne Bihari ji ke raas ko dekh liya ho, wo is sansaar me reh kar kya karega?*[33]' concluded the guide to which no one dared argue except for exchanging amused glances.

---

[32] Is this the season of Krsna going on here?
[33] One who has witnessed the divine dance, why will he bother to live in this world?

Meera lingered to thoroughly observe the interiors of the room - something pulling her into the whole story of Radha Krsna grooming each other for the *raas*. What must it be like to perform *raas* with the God himself who epitomised attraction, charm, art and music?

She was still unsatisfied on the subject of Radha's significance and the local priests did not shed much light, often looking at her with reproach when she questioned too much. Who is this mystical Radha? If she is the divine consort, then why did the Lord not marry her? And some say that she was already married and much elder to Krsna when she met him for the first time. How do we reconcile such a relation with today's moral context?

Seeing her come up with the same question about Radha every time, Sumer sat next to her when they took a tea break at a small roadside shop in between the temple visits. The dilapidated little hut cum shop was run by an old woman who sold tea to visitors. She was kind enough to brew a fresh potion of sugarless tea for Meera and her family. This trick of asking for sugarless tea always worked because it ensured that a fresh pot would be made.

'Do you know what Radha means?' asked Sumer to which Meera shook her head.

'In Yugandhar, Shivaji Savant says that *Ra* means attaining something and *Dha* means moksha. So Radha essentially could mean someone who wants to attain moksha.'

She was now hooked and stared curiously at her father, 'But that could be anyone, that could be me, no?'

'Exactly. Interestingly, no scriptures really go deep into Radha's description or story. One way to look at it might be to see Radha as an ideal devotee who is seeking liberation through consummate devotion.'

She let the thought sink in and nodded silently.

'Few others try to describe her as a *shakti* of Krsna. See, when the Supreme Lord created the universe, his authorities and powers to execute different functions were manifested as different forms of 'shakti'. For e.g. His power of creativity was deified as Saraswati and so on. Shakti became the fountain of primordial cosmic energy that creates, catalyses changes as well as destroys. And you could reconcile this interpretation with the other one because as Sri Ram says in Ramcharitmanas,

Samdarsi mohi kah sab kou, sevak priy ananyagati sou

It means - Although I'm known to be impartial, the devotee remains my most favorite because he depends on no one else but me. The point being that Lord is controlled by no one but his devotee. By letting yourself be controlled by him, you become a devotee and in turn, you now control the Almighty himself. So a true devotee is, in essence, also a *shakti* of Lord. Thus, Radha could be the perfect devotee as well as his energy.'

Sumer smiled on watching her eyes brighten. 'Now, don't bother more priests in the rest of the temples.'

She chuckled, 'You could have explained this earlier.'

'You didn't ask.'

Meera was briefly taken aback at the truth of that statement. The one thing that she had always found hard was to ask, be it for help or favor or support. She wondered if her burdens could have been lighter if she could just...ask.

Thus concluding the topic and their visits in Vrindavan, Sumer got up and led the group to their next destination, Gokul which was a bit further by road and needed an SUV. Meera delightfully followed, almost skipping like a twelve year old and holding the hand of her father whom she loved more than anyone else in this world.

****

In a couple of hours, after visiting Gokul and Raman Reti, they arrived on the precinct of Nandgram temple that stood aloft at Nandiswara Hill.

'We completed the *parikrama* - all 21km,' said Kavita like a child eager to gather accolades after finishing her homework.

'In how much time?' came the reply from the guide so casually that it hurt the pride of Kavita.

'Around seven hours.'

The guide smiled disparagingly as if his pre-conceived notion of what the tourists were capable of had been proven right once again. The locals finished it in three hours.

The guide showed to them, the temple itself, the big courtyard and few small rooms that were claimed to be Nand baba's kitchen. Stories flowed incessantly and were beginning to sound similar to the ones they had heard in Gokul. Meera dallied behind, trying to peek into the kitchen curiously through the barred door. She could barely see anything in the dark room lined with heavy black stones. Once it would have been full of dairy products targeted by the scurrying boys in the house.

She caught up with her group on the huge wide terrace running around the courtyard. It provided a majestic view of the village and nearby areas down the hill.

'That's the road to Mathura that was taken by Krsna ji and he never came back,' the guide was pointing towards one of the roads that was running below. Meera's eyes followed it as it went further into the distance.

She took a circular route to look at the stretch of lands expanding in all directions beneath the hill. Apparently, life had not advanced much from the yesteryears. The tiny rudimentary cottages had somehow kept themselves untouched from much of the modern innovations. The luster had gone without finding a suitable replacement as if the land refused to be identified by anything but the deity that had mercilessly left it in pursuit of his duty.

As they descended the narrow alleys from atop, Meera noticed the locks hanging on most of the houses. The abodes are too small for the growing needs of people and for the lack of expansion possibilities, their inhabitants had probably found better suited and fitted homes elsewhere. Soon the family had resumed their seats in the SUV and was ready to continue the journey.

Using photography as an excuse, Meera carefully made the vehicle stop just at the juncture where the road to Mathura started. She got out of the vehicle with her bulky SLR camera, took a few steps on the road and turned to look at the entrance to Nandgram. This is where Krsna had taken his leave. This was the marred lane which had seen the footsteps of God crossing one-way in an outbound direction. Remembering her pretext, she closed one eye and embraced the camera with the other. She kept staring as the scene transformed in a bygone era.

The dusty road abuzz with Krsna's loved ones must have kissed its Lord's feet one last time - the whole of Vrij *mandal* standing to look at him as he left on a fatal mission to meet Kansa.

Both her eyes closed in answer to an inner calling. The earth trembled with the footsteps of thousands of inhabitants of Nandgram, Vrindavan, Gokul and the entire Vrij *mandal* - men and animals - anyone who had derived pleasure from Krsna's company.

Parthsaarthi ascended the chariot and stood up handsomely, radiating divinity all around - ready to take a leave so mercilessly from the mortals he had made ecstatic by his character and friendship. The crowd quivered feverishly at the thought of farewell and found little solace from the composure and steadfastness of their friend and savior. The goodbyes were not to be said, only expressed in tears as the chariot started moving.

Just for a moment, he looked back at his people with eyes brimming with love. Brijwasis had started running after the chariot and looking at the receding figure of their beloved with blurry and teary eyes. The road was soon laden with tired bodies of villagers whose eyes had still not accepted defeat. Meera looked at the entrance gate and saw a girl standing tranquil and looking in the direction Krsna had left. Her face was as radiant as that of Madhav

- wistful, tender and glorious. The very next moment, she appeared to be bigger than other girls crying next to her. As Meera realised, the girl's form was actually growing. And it continued to grow in dimension, making up for the distance between her and the chariot. As it grew, the face itself started to morph into that of Krsna. Soon, the figure expanded to encompass the whole sky and filled every pore in every direction. After kissing every particle of Brij bhoomi's atmosphere, the form dissolved and disintegrated like a *rangoli* washed with water.

Meera quietly opened her eyes and steadied herself. The reality in front brought her back to the present. Then she kneeled down and leaned back finding a perfect angle for balance as she often did while photographing. Holding her lens deftly in a firm grasp, she expertly clicked a few pictures at different levels and angles, knowing that no camera could capture what she had just witnessed.

She wished that her visions be etched permanently in her consciousness and may they never need any artificial memory card. Just before getting back up, she knew what she had to do - she lowered her fingers to caress the soil and then touched her heart. For all she cared, she had kissed the sapphire feet that had unflinchingly given up their past and walked on steadily to a higher purpose. From where she saw, those footsteps could still be seen, clearly seared into the heart of this land.

****

She hurried to join the others and an hour later, their caravan was speeding next to the mustard fields. Plush yellow flowers swaying in the mild wind as one sees in countless Bollywood movies lined both sides of the road. The sun had just begun retiring for the day and its slanted golden rays kissed the yellow buds making them glitter. Soon they had reached the final destination for the day - Radha Rani temple at Barsana. It was again a destination on a higher altitude and a few hundred steps separated the tired travelers from Laadli ji's mahal[34] on top of the hill.

---

[34] Radha ji's palace - laadli means favorite

As soon as she stepped inside the palace on top, the air made Meera feel alive and excited in a way she had never experienced before. The huge courtyard overlooking the village below was occupied by *kirtan mandli* members who were completely engrossed in singing and dancing to their rhythmic *bhajans*, and many spectators were occasionally pulled in to join the dance.

The hues of the setting sun, the drum beats, musical chanting and carefree dancing aligned in a way that transcended any orchestrated professional performance she had seen anywhere in the world. Yes, even the glorious Broadway shows - Lion King, Wicked - would pale in comparison to the ad hoc magic created by these few artists who had ascended to divinity in their art by some mystical incomprehensible logic-defying means.

Laadli ji sat watching from her small chamber as the palace was lit up in divinity and as devotees fell on her feet in a trance. Meera saw the same girl she had seen bidding farewell to Krsna - she was the queen here, she was smiling to her loyal devotees who would never cease to express their disapproval of the enchanting cow herder, who had left their darling behind to pine after him. But Meera did not find her pining or remorseful, she found her glowing and smiling - the fountain of a bottomless energy.

The sun soon set and the maroon skies revealed a beautiful crescent of the moon. The family decided to spend some more time in the temple quadrangle before calling it a night. Meera strolled to a corner and sat down.

When was the last time she had felt so tranquil and so enchanted? Funny that she thought of the word enchanted - but isn't it great to be able to feel and believe in magic? Even if this feeling is an outcome of some stupid spell that binds this land, she would love to submit to that spell. Oh, what a sad life it must be that doesn't believe in some kind of magic.

Then, she laughed at her own thought. She was that person, that non-believer just few months ago who had given up on life.

Yet she was here tonight enjoying nothing but the vastness of sky, the spirit of a piece of land, the charm of a stone statue that smiled at her mysteriously and music of some hippies, because tonight she had the eyes that saw stars, faith, devotion and magic in them.

She wanted to believe in every tale and every vision. Yes probably right now, Krsna was braiding Radha's hair and the *gopis* were putting on their *kajal*. They would be stepping out in the garden soon and Krsna would start playing the flute - the divine melody that would soon flood everybody's consciousness with pure love and devotion. Every *gopi* would have her own Krsna and Krsna would have his own Radha. The divine dance would follow till they joined in unison like a dark cloud and a milky lightening - it would be hard to distinguish who was who. And then, at the onset of the dawn, Madhusudan would return to the Baanke Bihari temple, leaving his *raj*[35] on the *chaukhat*[36].

Meera smiled uncontrolled, her lips widening to show more teeth than she ever had before. If she was going mad, this was definitely one of the telltale signs.

****

Meera added another entry to her diary that night.

The best stories come perhaps from the tortured souls.

I do not know if God exists but to live a life thinking He doesn't seems futile and worthless, more importantly, purposeless. If I knew anything of morality or ethics, the greatest sin would be to live a purposeless life. I refuse to do that. I thought I had always believed in Him and perhaps I did. But I have only felt His presence strongly now - probably because I feel it's responsible for healing my shattered being. And the fact that something so badly damaged could be healed proves the existence of a power of incredible nature - one that can restore. Time heals but it always leaves a scar behind. Only a true restorative power can ease you of the pain and the scar. In a

---

[35] dust
[36] door frame

religious calling, I find the shreds of such a power. In a spiritual journey, I find its manifestation full-blown and matured. In a heightened sense of self-awareness, I have seen it blooming within my self. Its seed hibernates within us all, waiting to be germinated with water of faith. In most cases, that's where it keeps lying and dies if not nurtured.

Somewhere along life, as I became embroiled in existing, I forgot I wanted to live first. Thirty years of my life have been spent and I am, fortunately or unfortunately, at a point where I can ask questions that seem important. As I question, seek, ponder restlessly and feel the dimension of time beneath my running feet, I smile and I cry. I smile when I ask the question that makes me feel I am at least at a higher plane of awareness than I was ever before. I cry when I find an answer that resonates with the new me.

To an educated, progressive and practical mind, I might be traveling in a direction opposite to evolution. To God, I hope I'm traveling toward. Ironical - because I believe God is omnipresent, so I'm perhaps traveling in a circle. Or, may be that it doesn't matter where I'm traveling to because I'm bound to encounter Him. To see Him alone may be more than enough, to feel Him might be divine, I hope I can assimilate Him.

What were my pains if not my fears of the unknown? There exist all parallels and superlatives of any pain I have felt or could ever feel. Men have survived those, so who am I to complain of a tough life? Would I rather have a life cushioned with predictable rites but hollow on the inside? If not, then what right do I have to complain?

****

It was time to bid farewell to the sacred land. After paying a last visit to the Baanke Bihari temple and bowing respectfully to the flag on its top, the group proceeded to the railway station. Sumer explained, 'It symbolises asking the Lord to facilitate our next visit.'

Soon, everyone had taken their places in the railway coach as the train left from Mathura. Meera sneaked to occupy the side seat in front of Sumer and started watching the scenery moving outside the blurry window glass. The tired members soon dozed off.

Sumer looked at Meera indulgently, 'You have been asking lots of questions on Krsna.'

'Yeah, I am your daughter, no? Just as inquisitive,' she smiled back.

'Dad,' she started what she had been long wanting to do - talk heart-to-heart with her father. It's ironic how difficult it can be, at times, to open your heart to people you are really close with. She knew her father was the best guide possible to lead her out of her disquiet but she never had the courage to talk to him about her real feelings or fears for she could not afford to let him see through her pains. Plus, parents always have an emotional bias. Sumer might have been an excellent mentor to someone else but his judgments and thoughts would always be biased when it came to his precious daughter. This is why even the most acclaimed surgeons never operate on their family members themselves.

'Yes, sweetheart,' he said looking above the newspaper spread out in his hands.

'I did not know what to expect from this trip but I'm glad I came.'

'I know you don't believe in rituals, worship and such forms of faith and that is completely fine. But you are very spiritual just like your Dad - never forget that,' he replied.

She always felt that fathers and daughters have a very special connection. She had heard Sumer say this to a friend long ago when she was just a teenager -

"There is not enough time to love our daughters, they go away sooner than we can imagine. So, I try to spend as much time with her as I can."

Somehow, she never forgot that. Neither did she forget the steadiness with which he sent her away when the time came - unflinchingly, yet lovingly - as only Dads can. As time passed, she saw lesser and lesser of him. That hurt her and she hoped he missed her as much as she missed him. But to let go is another herculean task that only Dads have the strength for. She felt he must have been disappointed in her after her failures but gradually she realised that he had never lost trust in her and instead of making her recover on a superficial bed of reassurances, he infused a strength that no one could take away. And, he had been doing it all along, silently.

Amidst such fond thoughts for her Dad, the gentle rocking motion of the train induced that inescapable lethargy in Meera which made her eyelids grew heavier and heavier.

PART THREE

Chapter FOURTEEN
City of Justice

Somewhere in the City of Justice...

Two massive pillars of gold stood majestically at each of the six gates of this mystical city, connected in an arch in the shape of the Sun - its rays designed with lustrous gemstones of unseen colors and shades. Below the arch on each gate was written the same message -

" | Son of Vivaswata welcomes you | "

Upon entering the northernmost gate, a long walk on the wide pathway surrounded by lush green gardens took one to a palatial structure covered with jewels and refined decorations. Inside, in a big chamber of white solid walls and pillars, a man was sitting on a huge desk - his head bent over a thick hard bound book. His desk was full of similar thick journals neatly stacked in multiple columns. The room was lined with thick golden accents. Two people arrived at the entrance to this chamber but stood unnoticed for the next twenty minutes. Only when the man on the table closed his journal did one of the newcomers speak with a noticeable bow of his head - 'Sir Chitragupta.'

The man looked up carefully at the other newcomer. He was still making his observations when the other person continued, 'This is Meera. She is the new intern...'

The sentence was cut short by an impatient interruption from the man, 'We are not accepting any interns currently, Bhanudas.'

'She was sent by Vaasudev, Sir Chitragupta.'

The weight of the reference was not lost upon the man as he stood up at his desk gently. Any hints of surprise were quickly replaced with a reverent acknowledgment for the name that had been pronounced. Meera's companion, Bhanudas, stepped forward to hand a scroll to him. For the first time, Meera got an opportunity to look fully at the powerful accountant whose reputation preceded him. He was a healthy looking, medium height man with deep-set discerning eyes that sized up anything and everything that entered his field of vision. His indigo blue kurta and white dhoti made him starkly conspicuous in the bright room.

Chitragupta read the scroll carefully and stamped his seal on it before handing it back. He finally spoke with a soft look in his eyes, 'Welcome to the City of Justice, Meera. You are one of the rare few interns who have crossed these doors and you are following a lineage more distinguished than you can imagine. Bhanudas will accompany you throughout your day today and guide you in your journey. You are here to only observe, so don't do anything you are not told to. You can ask questions but Bhanudas is not obliged to answer. Your internship begins now and will end at sunset.'

As Chitragupta stopped giving the set of instructions, Bhanudas spoke with deference, 'Which project, my Lord?'

'Karma.'

Bhanudas bowed and was quickly followed out by Meera. They went out together leaving Chitragupta staring at Meera with a mix of incomprehension and geniality.

Chapter FIFTEEN

Internship

She followed Bhanudas through a long corridor before he entered a small room. He pointed at a cupboard on the right and said, 'Please wear the dress assigned for interns. It is to ensure we don't get stopped at each security check post.'

In fifteen minutes, Meera came out donning her new uniform - a white kurta with golden lining and a cyan chooridar. Next, she followed Bhanudas out in a big courtyard. She had still not grasped her new surroundings well and looked at everything with curiosity of a toddler. She had never seen anything quite like this. The ground had no soil and was filled with bluish crystals that grew copious amounts of trees and grass. Not a single blighted leaf could be sighted and while the shades of green varied in the foliage, its brightness and glow remained uniformly sanguine. It was hard to place the city with its conflicting old fashioned decor and apparently advanced looking infrastructure. Bhanudas asked her to sit on a bench in the middle of the courtyard, while he sat down opposite her. He opened a scroll and Meera peeked at it curiously.

'Meera, I have your schedule,' he began. 'We will begin with the Journal Grid.'

'Um, excuse me but can I ask where we are?' asked Meera with an innocent expression that said "Please, first things first."

Bhanudas was surprised briefly but then smiled at the obviousness of the question. 'I thought you knew. We are in the City of Justice or Dharmapuri as you might like to call it. Better yet, Yamapuri, we are in Yamapuri.'

Meera's eyes widened - 'Yamapuri? Have I died?'

Bhanudas replied simply, 'Please have some patience. Your time has not come yet. You will understand it all very soon.'

If it wasn't for the harmony of her surroundings and the agreeable nature of her companion, she might have persisted in asking further.

Bhanudas got up and walked to the corner where a stack of cloud shaped things were kept. Meera followed. With a flick of his wrist, he summoned one of the cloud objects that came floating in front of him. He casually stepped into it and gestured Meera to do the same. Hiding her surprise, she stepped up on it and was still looking for something to hold on to as the object started moving ahead. Fortunately, it glided so smoothly that any hint of motion came only from the receding scenery in the surroundings.

'This is our cloud transportation system, it travels on the direction of the mind. The advanced versions travel on the speed of the mind as well,' explained Bhanudas to her amusement. She was only familiar with cloud storage so far but apparently, she was in a more advanced land.

'What does it mean to travel at the speed of mind?'

He smiled, 'It means that you reach wherever you want instantaneously.'

Their slower than mind cloud vehicle soon reached a building that extended infinitely in height. She read the welcome sign that said, 'Journal Grid, only authorized personnel can enter.' After clearing the security, Bhanudas took her inside the door. It was only upon entering this room that Meera realised that the building extended the same infinite length in depth as well. The room was an endless grid with endless rows and columns. Every column had innumerable cells.

Soon, they found themselves on another cloud shaped vehicle conjured upon Bhanudas's will that started floating up and down and left and right through the grid space.

'This is the journal grid where all record keeping happens.'

'Record of?'

'Karma index,' came the answer so obviously that Meera did not know whether to risk appearing foolish by asking more questions or submit to her curiosity and ask them nonetheless. In the confusion, she did neither.

Bhanudas made the vehicle stop in front of a cell in the grid where a man sat looking at the screen in front with a serious expression. His head had three green cords attached to it and the other end of the wires united and went into another tablet like device on the right. The cell space was tiny with just enough space for the man and the equipment. Meera realised that the screen was only visible at one angle as Bhanudas fine-tuned the position of their cloud vehicle. She saw that the screen was playing a scene where an Indian woman was shouting at her maid for breaking a glass.

The man kept watching the screen continuously while Bhanudas explained, 'He is watching the actions of that living creature and his mind decodes the actions into karma entries which emerge as new lines on the tablet. Each entry consists of the description of the action in a standard form and a value associated with that action. This value is added to the karma index of this living being in the next system.'

'Just like financial accounting?'

'Yes, except that this one matters,' he replied in a matter-of-fact manner.

Next, he took her to a few different cells where she saw different living beings being watched incessantly by different workers - including an Indian child, an American girl, a Japanese woman, a bird in the Amazon and a spider in Malaysia. Every consequential action was traced and recorded meticulously without a miss.

'This must be a tedious job!' she exclaimed looking at the utter concentration with which the workers in the cell kept track of every action that took place in the universe.

'Yes, the workers work in five hour shifts and are replaced by a fully energised batch. We have four such batches in our current setup. The master system assigns the living creatures to these workers through a previously designed algorithm. These are highly trained workers and it takes us lot of time to train new ones. We are currently working to automate the whole process so that the workers can be sent back to Indrapuri from where they come.'

Despite running high and low vertically, Meera had seen no end to the grid which ensured that she could not estimate the count of all the living beings on earth. As they were whizzing past the grid, her eyes caught a weird looking creature on one of the screens.

'Who was that? I have never seen anything like that,' she asked Bhanudas.

'Let me correct you. You have not seen anything like that *on earth.*'

Meera only kept staring silently. She was no longer thinking of counting the cells, she knew it would be a futile exercise.

****

The next destination was the building known as Office of Transaction. As they entered the door, a huge but finite hall greeted them. It was fitted with a humongous monitor in front that contained hundreds of thousands of tiny individual screens. Each screen displayed a series of characters and symbols that kept changing fast.

'The outputs from the journal grid feed into the system in front and the karma index is recalculated for each living being as new entries are processed.'

'That weird string is the karma index?'

Bhanudas nodded.

'And what's the small code on top of that string?'

'That is the unique identification code of the living being.'

Her eyebrows shot up in admiration before she remembered something. 'But those are not enough screens to account for all living beings.'

Bhanudas smiled and flicked his neck sideways. And doing so, a new page got turned on the monitor as the symbols changed. The screens displayed the information on the next set of living beings.

'Impressive.'

Meera watched the screens for some time and started noticing different patterns. 'Why are some symbols not changing? What does that mean?'

'It means that living being has died within the last two hours, so the karma index is not going to change until...'

'Until?'

'Until it is reborn.'

This was the first time that Meera realised she was discussing a religious topic. But she had also noticed the time duration that he had mentioned. She could not help asking incredulously, 'So one gets reborn within two hours?'

'Yes, that is our policy. We can discuss it when we visit the dome of death. And there's another possibility for the symbol not changing briefly.'

'That no new action took place?'

'Logically yes but that is highly unlikely because living beings cannot survive without performing actions. Even breathing is an action. No, the only other way symbol does not change is that the new actions are non-transactional.'

'Please elaborate,' implored Meera.

'Transaction means facing the consequences of your karma. Transacting a karma means living through its effects. Every living being has to transact all of its karma.'

'But you said some actions are non-transactional, so one doesn't have to face the consequences of such actions?'

'Right. Any action dedicated to God or done with the intention of assimilating in the One does not add to your karma index.'

Lines were appearing on Meera's forehead as she began connecting the dots in her mind. 'Why is karma index so important anyway?'

'Because that is one of the only two things that is in control of a living being on its journey to the ultimate destination?'

Meera's eyebrows shot up on hearing those words. 'What? What is our ultimate destination? And what do we control besides karma?'

Bhanudas smiled. 'The only other thing you control is your faith. And your goal is to go back to where you came from. To merge in your original source. To free yourself from the illusion. To unite with the One.'

'Moksha?'

'I believe that is what humans like to call it,' replied Bhanudas with a smile.

She had so many questions that none came out of her mouth.

He pointed his finger at another screen in the middle of the monitor. 'Do you look at that index symbol glowing in green? That symbol stands for the number zero. That is what your destination is,' he said with a broad smile. 'Towards zero.'

'Towards zero,' repeated Meera as if in trance.

'Let's go,' pronounced Bhanudas.

They had turned around to leave when Meera saw a single screen fitted on the left side of the door with a touch keyboard. Bhanudas followed her gaze and took her to the screen. 'It is the lookup monitor.'

'May I?' asked Meera to which he nodded.

She punched in the symbols she had in mind. Bhanudas laughed for the first time. Meera looked at him and smiled before turning back to see what the screen was going to reveal. She saw a middle aged Indian man in a simple looking room that appeared to be some kind of an office. He was working patiently on the files in front of him. From the appearance of his clothes and desk, he did not seem to be someone on a high rank. As a puzzled look started to cover her expressions, Bhanudas tactfully interjected, 'Not what you expected, huh? How does this insignificant man attain the zero stage?'

She looked at him as he read her mind flawlessly and nodded in assent.

'He is a widower, his children are comfortably settled abroad and send him money time to time but he doesn't use any of it. He works sincerely, goes back home, cooks a simple meal for himself, prays and goes to sleep. He helps anyone he can but since he is suffering from partial paralysis in one leg, cannot do much running around.'

'If he is so good and apparently among the rare few who have reached the elusive zero, why does he have to suffer?'

'What is suffering?'

'I think paralysis should qualify for suffering.'

Bhanudas smiled. 'Remember Tulsidas, Surdas, Paramhansa? Do you know what terrible ordeals they went through?'

'Great point and they devoted their whole life to God! This is what God gave them?'

'They reached zero index too, God gave them exactly what they wanted.' With this statement, Bhanudas opened the door and stepped out waiting for Meera to follow.

She was agitated at not understanding so many things and decided to display her unrest openly. 'How can anyone want paralysis or sickness or blindness?'

'No. They did not want that but they did not ask to be cured either. They wanted liberation and that's what they got.'

Meera thought carefully. 'So, zero index is liberation...What about positive index? Is that better?'

'No, it's not better than zero, nothing is better than zero. If you have a non-zero index, you will keep getting re-born.'

'Ah!'

'But positive is better than negative. You will be rewarded for your positive karma in your life and have to suffer for the negative ones.'

'What's a reward?'

'It is whatever you desired while accumulating the positive karma. Your *bhavna* behind doing those actions will determine your reward. A man doing good to become rich will get reward in form of material richness, Mirabai got it in the form of union with her Lord and so on.'

'One might enjoy the material rewards and keep doing positive karma only - why bother liberating?'

'So, you are now ready for our next destination.'

****

The next destination was a garden more beautiful than words could express. The soft grass filled the expanse decorated with trees and flowers that Meera had never seen before. The scent of exotic fragrances filled the air. After walking Meera up to the center where a beautifully carved fountain was located, Bhanudas sat down on a stone seat facing towards Meera who was still looking all around in awe.

'What is beauty?'

'A thing like this which makes you wonder how looking at something can give one such joy.'

'Who are you?'

'I am Meera Sachdev...'

'What if I tell you, you are also Gayatri Desai, Ethan Finn, Nikolo Ustinov, Deborah Sanders and many more...'

Meera had for the first time, started feeling uncomfortable under Bhanudas's penetrating eyes. 'I don't know what to say.'

When Bhanudas got up, she could hardly believe her eyes. She exclaimed, 'How have you become so tall all of a sudden!'

'Doesn't matter.' He blinked his eyes and got back to his previous height. He blinked again and the garden in which they were sitting transformed into a barren desert.

Meera swirled around a full circle to make sure she was actually standing in an endless scorching desert. 'Stop!'

'I see I'm scaring you. Please pardon me but I'm just making a point. What do you hear?'

'The faint sound of the wind.'

Bhanudas gently flicked his neck and asked, 'Now?'

She tried listening more intently with a puzzled look on her face. 'Still the same.'

'It's not audible to your human ears. Let me give you the hearing capability of a bat.' He again blinked and suddenly Meera jumped on hearing a shrill sound. She immediately covered her ears with her hands. 'Yes I can hear it now!' she said in a loud voice.

Bhanudas smiled and made the sound stop. 'Why are you shouting?' he added with a smile.

'Ok, what exactly is going on? What's your point?'

'I'm glad you asked. The point is that you see what your eyes can perceive, you hear what your ears can detect. What you think you are seeing, hearing, smelling and sensing is merely an illusion.'

'So, this garden is an illusion.'

'No, everything. Me, universe, your home, your parents, your body - everyone. Except for the One.'

Seeing Meera lost in thoughts and perturbed, he continued, 'When Abhimanyu was killed in Mahabharat, Arjun completely lost his composure and it looked like he would not be able to fight anymore. So Krsna took him to the heaven where Abhimanyu had reached after his death. Upon seeing his son, Arjun rushed forward to hug him and expressed his grief. Abhimanyu politely told him that the relationship of father and son between them only existed on earth and after death, that bond no longer holds any meaning. That's when the reality dawned upon Arjun, that's when he truly understood what Krsna meant by illusion. Let's walk.'

They started walking through the sand. In a few minutes, a caravan on camels could be seen at some distance. 'Those who seek truth have found it even in deserts, you know,' added Bhanudas with a smile. The confounded Meera followed the caravan with her gaze as it vanished farther away. 'But that's not Hinduism!'

She had barely finished her sentence as the whole scene transformed to an urban setting. She could hardly recognize Bhanudas in a classic black suit. 'Which setting do you prefer?'

Meera had understood the message he was trying to convey. She replied, 'Doesn't matter.'

He nodded and they found themselves back in the City of Justice where they had begun. They were standing in middle of a big town square. 'That was the Ignis Fatuus, commonly known as Maaya Mahal.'

Meera nodded silently and was lost in thoughts.

'You still think that man is suffering?'

'No, I understand that he sees things for what they are. Unlike myself.'

Bhanudas looked up and said, 'Your senses can deceive you but your faith will not. What you believe is up to you. Do not tie it to your senses.'

'So, why am I alive? Is there a purpose to all this? I'm sorry but after seeing all this, I don't know if it's worth living or not.'

'I think Satyapoorna can give you a better answer for that.'

Chapter SIXTEEN

Four: Conversation of Purpose

Bhanudas dropped Meera off at a white building that stood conspicuously undecorated in its surroundings. 'I will wait outside.'

She went in through the door and found herself in a magnificent big hall that was all empty except for two wooden chairs in the middle. A woman entered at the other end from another door on the left and started walking towards the chairs. Meera also moved forward to meet her. As she looked at her from a close distance, she found her to be a pleasant looking composed woman whose age could be guessed only by few faint lines at the corner of her eyes and lips. She was dressed in an all white saree and wore her hair neatly pinned up. She gestured to Meera to take a seat.

'Hi Meera, how are you?'

'I am very well, thanks.'

'My name is Satyapoorna, the fulfiller of truth,' the woman added with the trace of a smile.

'Nice to meet you. Your home is very simple and empty.'

'Truth needs no adornments, does it?'

'No. And you can help me understand the truth?'

'Well, I am your own truth. I am the truth that lies within you but is still to be revealed. So what I tell to anyone depends on what lies within her and how much is she capable of understanding.'

'I'm sorry but I don't understand. What is my truth? Isn't truth absolute? How can it vary from person to person?'

'That is what you think but truth comes from knowledge and knowledge is inherent in everyone. When we say we *know*, we simply mean we have *discovered* that piece of knowledge that already lay covered within our soul. We have the infinite library of the universe in our own minds. Newton did not discover gravitation from some external flash of knowledge, it was all there in his mind. Some are able to tap it better and others not so much.'

Meera was taken in by the novel concept propounded by the wise lady in front of her. 'What is my truth? What can I know?'

For the first time, Satyapoorna laughed. 'You cannot expect me to unleash the infinite knowledge in a flash but the gist is simple. You know the truth once you understand the illusion. What remains after you remove the illusion is the only truth.'

'So everything and everyone is an illusion. But for whom we refer to as the One or God...'

'Yes and we carry a part of God in ourselves - that is the truth we carry.'

'Our soul?'

'Yes or *Atman* as I like to call it. If *Brahman* is the One, then *Atman* is His representation within each being. *Brahman* is the absolute and only truth that exists - it is the supreme soul. *Atman* is the eternal essence within us, it is our individual soul that came from the *Brahman*. That is all there is to know.'

'But why did *Brahman* produce *Atman*?'

'That I cannot tell you because it is beyond your perception and I cannot see beyond your perception.'

'But you said we know everything.'

'Everything that you can perceive and understand. Some things are beyond the logic of mortals. This is why we have faith - belief in something that we cannot even understand.'

'But knowing that everything is nothing but an illusion, why should I live? What should be my objective?'

'You should live because it gives you an invaluable opportunity to attain the true goal. The human body is the perfect vehicle to work towards that goal. Action is your only option. Your ultimate objective is to unite with *Brahman* - a concept known as moksha. The only pursuit worth venturing is to try to liberate your soul.'

'And how does that happen?'

'I believe you are now familiar with the concept of karma and its index. Only when one does not have any more karmas left to transact, can the soul be liberated. Do the karma such that it will help you in reaching that goal.'

'What kind of karma are those?'

'Not what kind of karma but the kind of *intention* with which any karma is done. Any action that you dedicate to God is a non-transactional karma. You can do anything as long as you do it with pure dedication to God. Whatever you do, do it for the One and you won't have to carry any karma value from it. It won't add anything to your karma index and eventually you will reach the elusive zero.'

'Is that how the old man had reached zero? He basically dedicated all actions selflessly to God?'

'Yes. He has already transacted all his previous karmas and since he is not accumulating any more karma through any of his new actions, he is at zero now. If he continued like this, he shall be liberated.'

'That sounds simple but I'm sure it's not else more people would have been able to do that. You said one can dedicate any karma to God. Even bad ones?'

'Yes.'

'So, I can get away with murder if I dedicate it to God?'

'As ridiculous as it might sound to you, yes you can. Think it like this. Who is the person who actually executes the capital punishments? Isn't it the executioner?'

'Yes.'

'Does he get punished for those murders?'

'No.'

'Because it is understood that he is not doing it for himself. Similarly, if one is truly able to dedicate any action selflessly to God, he will not have to transact it. Period. If you can do a murder for no selfish reason and dedicate it to God in a pure sense, yes you might still be hanged for it in the society but you will not accumulate any negative karma for it.'

Meera sat quietly to let the pithy sermons be absorbed by her mind before asking, 'Why don't we stop doing anything then? That will make our balance zero.' She thought she had finally found a loop hole in the cycle of karma.

Satyapoorna smiled. By wave of her hand, she produced a small device in her hand that had a small screen. She turned it around so that Meera could take a look at it - it was a string of symbols like Meera had seen before.

'It is the karma index of someone,' said Meera.

'Yes, it is your index.'

Meera's eyes lit up at the same time her eyebrows went up in anxiety. She had badly wanted to look at that but was feeling too timid to ask Bhanudas. But she soon realized how futile it was since she did not know how to decode it to decimal digits.

Satyapoorna observed her for some time before speaking, 'The only thing you should watch is how this string changes. Since you are here, none of your actions here were adding to your index. But let me temporarily put you in the earthen state so that your actions start affecting your index.'

'Ok...'

'As you proposed, you can try stopping all your actions and let's see how easily you can control your karma index. You can start now.'

First ruffled, then distraught with the sudden challenge posed by her companion, Meera started to quieten her activities in an effort to relax. But to her amazement the string started changing - the more she tried to control its movement, the more it moved. After couple of minutes, Satyapoorna put down the monitor and told her that the experiment was over.

'Why do you think you still accumulated karma when physically you were doing nothing?'

'Breathing?...'

'Yes to a small extent but mostly because your mind was active, your thoughts and intentions were still running and they add to your karma index as well. The crux is that it is impossible for us to do no karma because karma is not just any physical activity, it includes the activity of the mind too. If the mind is active with the idea of egoism or forced inactivity, then it is action in inaction. One who uses such argument to sit idle and think that he will attain salvation is merely naive and lazy.'

Meera sat silently for long. She realized that Satyapoorna never blinked and her presence was somewhat daunting. 'Just like truth is daunting at times,' she thought to herself.

'Is that all I need to know?' asked Meera without expecting a simple answer.

'Yes.'

Both of them got up and Meera took her leave.

As Meera walked out, she found Bhanudas waiting patiently outside.

'How did you like her?'

'She was very helpful and wise.'

'Good, she comes from within you. If you liked her, it means you like who you are,' he added genially. 'How healthy did she look?'

Meera thought that was a weird question and her frown betrayed her thoughts.

'Oh, I am asking because the healthier she looked to you, the more truth you have within yourself.'

Meera was too dumbfounded to say anything to that.

****

'This is the southernmost gate into the city and it is very special,' said Bhaudas as they stood before a closed gate that resembled the one through which Meera had entered the city earlier. But she noticed two differences - it was closed and had no handle to open it. In fact, it was a solid slab of wood and not a pair of doors. She looked at Bhanudas with a perplexity that was well anticipated by him. He led her to the small platform built in front of the gate and blinked. The platform started moving down like an elevator. After few seconds, Meera found herself at what seemed like the basement level. As soon as it stopped and she followed Bhanudas out on a bridge like structure, she saw the huge river that was gushing with black water right below them.

'This is Vaitarani river - the carrier of sinners,' said Bhanudas looking at the water.

Upon noticing carefully, Meera felt a chill down her spine. She could see various living beings floating in the water crying for help. Their expressions and pleas for help alone inspired such misery that she found herself trembling.

'This is the only way sinners enter this city upon their death.'

To brake her surge of horrendous thoughts, she asked, 'And how about the good ones?'

'They are welcome through all other gates.'

'Where are they all going?'

'Dome of Death. Let's check it out.'

They crossed the bridge to the other side and entered another elevator. Meera could feel the elevator not just going up but moving sideways too, like an electrical car. When the door opened next, they came out into the open air.

Dome of Death - said the plain sign that stood in front of a big grey steel structure that resembled the inverted bowl. Somehow, Meera found her footsteps growing heavier as they reached the entrance. She did not know what to expect and seeing the plight of creatures floating in the black river of sin had already shaken her. For all she knew, she probably stood very close to the physical hell. And she did not even want to know what wretchedness unfolded in there.

'Come on,' said Bhanudas in a hurried manner and Meera walked faster to enter the dome. They had to walk down a lot of steps before they reached a platform where there were railway tracks on either side. But what had already caught Meera's attention were the seats on the platform and the people who occupied them - they were the bodies of the dead and looked pale. There were different expressions on their faces - tidy to disheveled, reposing to agitated, quiet to kvetching. Trains kept coming on both sides and random bodies descended from the trains on the left and stepped on to the ones going on the right, obviously in an opposite direction. But it could not have been random, Meera thought.

As if he had read her thoughts, Bhanudas started explaining, 'The souls come here to be sent to their new clothes, I mean bodies.'

'How is their new body selected?'

'Once they die, based on their karma index, they arrive in the city either through the river of sin or through the gates. After transacting their major sins or good actions, they are brought here. Their remaining karma index determines the body they will get - it can be any of the eighty four lac species we have. The higher your karma index, more likely you are to get a human body. And further higher it is, the more comfortable your life circumstances will be. I wish we had more time to show you the sophisticated system we run. You would have been amazed to see these trains from the inside where the hand-over happens,' said Bhanudas with a hint of child like pride in his voice that made Meera smile.

'I am confident that your system is utterly well built but I would rather not step inside those trains,' she replied with a suppressed shiver.

'Oh, I see.'

Chapter SEVENTEEN
Enlightenment

As they came back up to ground level, he looked up to observe something. Meera also followed his gaze and to her bewilderment, she saw two suns!

'What the,' she stopped herself on time. 'You have two suns?'

'Yeah, as of now. It is nearly the time. Your tour is about to end. You can spend some time in the Enlightenment Park and then you can have your parting meeting with Sir Chitragupta. This vehicle will take you to the park.'

'Oh,' exclaimed Meera upon knowing that she had only little time left in this weird place. She had just begun to understand some things and had already developed a liking for her trainer.

'I hope you are not leaving me. Would I see you again?'

'Of course, I will collect you from the park when it is time for the meeting. Have fun,' added Bhanudas while summoning a cloud car for Meera.

Meera was next headed to the park and she was curious to see what it could be. It sounded like some meditation place and she did not know how to proceed without any guidance, but she was underestimating her pre-programmed little vehicle. It knew where to take her. Once she entered, she was again proved wrong. Enlightenment Park was the last thing she expected in this uncanny place - it was actually like an amusement park and she could see tall structures that looked like rides!

****

Her route was already fed into the cloud and it took her to the first stop. It read 'The Big Bang' pointing to the surprisingly small looking building and she walked inside carefully. She wished she could go to the more exciting looking rides but hid her disappointment. There was one comfortable seat in the middle of the room which she took. As soon as she sat, the seat reclined and adjusted its height automatically. A belt was buckled and the seat began to slowly rotate. Meera was scared, but there was no going back. After few accelerated rotations, her eyes closed and when they opened she was stationary in space - yes big frickin' space with nothing around her. Was she floating in the universe?

'This is how your world started,' came the succinct announcement as the darkness around her filled with a light glow. 'Man often likes to question himself about how it all started and is disappointed when his logic fails to help him reach the answer. Since one cannot create something out of nothing, let us begin with the beginning. In the beginning, that something existed. That what existed when nothing else existed is I.'

Meera was awestruck by the sound and impact of the voice. She stopped her futile attempts to try spotting the unseen source and submitted herself to the surreal feeling of being in such a grand place.

'I existed in a formless entity - some call it *Brahman* or ether. I was everywhere and there was nothing that did not exist within me. I was calm. My energy lay latent and much time passed. But then, I decided to manifest myself in a tangible form. The reason is not important but that is how the world you came to know started. You might recognise it vaguely. Your science likes to call it the Big Bang.'

If a voice could smile, it would sound like that. The soothing voice finally helped Meera relax. As the story proceeded, she realised that if some point of intersection existed between religion and science, it couldn't be different than this. It couldn't be more fascinating than this. It made her happy that her faith in an unknown grand power, possibly the One who was apparently narrating this story, was so beautifully justified. She wanted to believe in His magnificence and every moment in this endless space made her feel His presence closely.

'Thus was born my Maaya, the physical illusion that you call universe. And I also created life and put myself in each living creature. Since then, man has been trying so hard to find a logical explanation for everything, but refusing to accept it on simple faith, something that could give him more answers. There are limits to his logic and I stand beyond that. Anyway,' continued the voice and Meera was hooked. 'Just like you sleep and wake up, this cosmos is manifested and then assimilated in me again and again - this cycle goes on and on.'

There was a vibration and Meera saw a tall, green flash of light appear in front.

'I sometimes take defined forms too but my form doesn't matter. I am everywhere and I am the only truth.'

As the voice faded away, a greenish glowing substance filled the space around her - it was neither liquid nor gas. After some time, it started quivering and accumulating at different places and voila! - shapes began to appear, transforming to stars, planets, galaxies, some things that we know and some that we don't know. Meera figured she was being given a demonstration of *The Creation* and she barely blinked as the events unraveled. Shapes in focus zoomed in automatically and the creation of life followed. As she watched, after the creation of life and full evolution, another vibration began through the green substance - everything started disintegrating. Soon, the shapes had decomposed back to the original substance and any trace of matter or energy was lost as the substance lay quiescent.

'And that is one cycle of creation and destruction. It lasts one *kalpa* - more than four billion years long. There have been millions of such cycles already.'

Meera was fascinated and overwhelmed - everything about her and her life seemed so tiny.

The light vanished and before she could react, Meera was transported back to the original small room. She could feel goose bumps as she stepped out of the chair.

****

The next stop filled her with excitement as she saw the big roller coaster set up with a board that read 'Fortune Ride'. 'What does it mean? Can it foretell my future?' wondered Meera as she stepped inside the door and headed towards the starting point of the ride. There was only one seat which she took hesitatingly. Next, the safety clasps were tightened and the chair moved ahead slowly. After advancing horizontally, visions started appearing in front of Meera out of thin air.

She saw herself laughing with a man and a baby - both their faces were out of sight. One thing that she could clearly see was the glow of happiness on her own face. She clasped the edge of her seat tightly as her chair inched to an ominous fall in its track. A loud scream went off as she fell down the drop in a near free fall. Finally, the chair slowly began ascending the next ramp. She had barely let the happiness from the previous flash sink in fully when the new imagery came up - it was her grandmother and she looked extremely ill. Her parents were sitting around her and she saw herself standing behind them. 'No!' came the instant reaction. 'Not Amma!' she cried out.

And then began the next fall - taller than the previous one. She screamed even louder this time. Soon, she had figured out the pattern - there was a vision on the ramps and then the intense falls. The visions varied from moments of happiness to utter pain. In less than ten minutes, she had seen a wide spectrum of severe feelings and by the time the ride reached its last few flashes, she neither felt affected by the auguries nor screamed during the falls.

She got out of the ride in a disheveled state.

'How was your ride?' came a mechanical kind of sound that Meera figured must be coming from an automated tape.

'It was as unpleasant as it could be,' she angrily muttered.

'Oh, I am sorry you didn't like it. I thought we showed some excellent prophecies. You seem more affected by the negative ones, is that so?'

Meera was nearly offended at the analysis and said nothing.

The voice continued, 'Perhaps it might have helped if we showed only one prophecy like you see in real life - one at a time.'

'Yes, maybe it would have been less confusing!'

'I see you prefer illusions.'

'What do you mean?'

'You prefer living one illusion at a time. You prefer riding between the highs and lows of your life so that you can keep crying or laughing over it. Mortals are funny creatures.' With that last amused sounding sentence, the voice dissolved away. She was still ruffled over the various visions and their meaning when she found Bhanudas waiting for her outside the park.

'Is this genuine? Was that my real future there?'

Bhanudas kept looking at her without saying anything. She suddenly felt a pang of embarrassment. Why was she worrying about things that were clearly an illusion? It made her feel as if nothing that she had seen so far had got into her tiny brain and she remained the ignorant fool that she was before.

Bhanudas replied to her thoughts, 'Don't be so hard on yourself. It takes time to practice what you have learned. And no, the ride isn't about showing you your future because that depends on your karma. It is exactly what it seemed - a roller coaster of emotions. You laugh, you cry and then some more as commanded by your senses and emotions.'

'But if I know that life is just an illusion and hence, all those visions don't matter, I don't suffer the ups and downs.'

'You said it!'

****

As they started their way back, they crossed a man - the first one that she had seen roaming on the ground. He wore a simple *dhoti* and a shawl wrapped elegantly and casually around his torso. His gait had a swagger-free command about it that made Meera wonder and gaze at him with regard. She saw a colony of green houses in a big area that stood out from other houses.

'What are those?'

'They are the abodes of some of the previous visitors, interns and research scholars.'

'Oh, can I see?' asked Meera. 'If you don't mind?' she added for formality's sake.

'Yes, I suppose we have some time,' replied Bhanudas while commanding their vehicle to change its direction by a wave of his hand.

'Why do you need to have their rooms? Do they revisit?'

'Yes, these are the privileged visitors who are given what you call the multiple entry visa,' said Bhanudas with a gleam in his eyes.

Meera smiled and got down to see the rooms. They all stood adjacent to each other joined by a common hallway. She softly opened the first door and peeked inside - it was a simple orderly room with hardly any traces of occupancy. But as she stepped inside, she spotted a simple round frame of glasses next to a diary on the desk. She almost jumped at what she saw next. It was a spinning yarn.

She hurried outside to where Bhanudas was standing, 'Isn't that...,' and she could barely finish. 'I can't believe it. Where's the stick though?'

'Well, he doesn't need that here. No one has the sick or weak bodies here.'

'So, why the glasses?'

'Oh, he likes those.'

'So, dead people can revisit in their bodies here?'

'We don't like to give any importance to dead bodies. For all that matters, the privileged souls can visit here in the bodies they choose. They normally take the form in the body in which they found their destination.'

Calling it out of the world was not a metaphor anymore and Meera did not know how to react. She merely shook her head, perplexed.

The next room was completely empty to her surprise. Before she could ask Bhanudas about the identity of its occupant, he himself ventured, 'It is Siddhartha's room. He doesn't keep anything.'

She found a white saree with thick blue borders in the next room. On the table were a rosary and a candle. Meera's eyes automatically closed in reverence at the sight.

By the time she was done visiting the first leg of rooms, she was trembling in awe. 'What am I doing here?' she wondered as she felt too small to be standing in the hallowed gallery.

Chapter EIGHTEEN
Chitragupta

The sky was turning bronze as Meera looked above. The bizarre view of two suns that were setting slightly apart in different phases captivated her gaze. She wasn't sure how many earth hours had passed, but she was sure that the day here was longer. Bhanudas took her back to the palace where they had first started the day. They ascended a bunch of beautifully carved stairs hanging in the air to reach the terrace where Chitragupta was, to her surprise, still working.

'I do like a change in the scene sometimes,' he said without resorting to any formal welcome.

Meera could feel that her thoughts were as audible as her spoken words and that did unsettle her momentarily, but then she reminded herself that she was on a land not governed by her earthly concerns and fears.

'Do you feel your visit is over?'

'Do I have the liberty of choosing when I think my visit is over?'

'No, but if you leave without attaining your purpose, that would be such a tragedy, isn't it?'

The man displayed no softness and Meera could feel in every word of his that she was not standing there by his choice. 'Why do you *not* want me to be here?'

Chitragupta looked up with a trace of admiration for the first time. 'Because you being here is an aberration in your cycle of karma and I don't like aberrations - it hampers my work.'

'Fair enough. As for your question, I don't think I understand the purpose fully. I had some very surreal experiences here and I don't know what to expect ahead. But I don't know if that is enough.'

Chitragupta further softened at her forthrightness. He clapped his hands and a person came up from behind with a tray and an exquisite looking vessel with two glasses. The person poured a golden liquid from the vessel into the glasses and handed one to both of them.

'We don't eat here but I think you will enjoy a sip of this solution.'

Meera hesitatingly took a sip and found the liquid to be tastelessly refreshing. Its aroma distinguished it from water. She gulped it down while Chitragupta sipped it at a leisurely pace.

'You know everything you needed to know and whatever was vaguely confusing for you should have been cleared here.'

'Thank you for letting me be here...'

She was cut off instantaneously by her interlocutor. 'Humility is good but your's borders on weakness! Why are you so timid?'

She was taken aback. 'Am I?'

'Don't you realise you never look in anyone's eyes? Right from your childhood, you never speak up even when you know the answer. Deference is good but not calling out the wrong does not make you pious!'

That cut right through her heart.

'But that discussion is not the objective here. People come here to have their faith rewarded and to realise that they should not abandon the search for their purpose. You shall find your truth if you continue seeking. Whatever you experienced here will help take the dust off your soul that blinds you to the reality.' He tilted the glass over his lips to finish off his drink.

'Vaasudev and I talked earlier after you left.' Meera could not help being amused at the casual reference - he made it sound like a simple meeting of two inconsequential friendly fellows.

He looked straight at her and continued, 'He wanted you to continue in your journey, that is why you are here.'

Meera felt an electric current through her on hearing that. In a trembling voice, she asked, 'Can I meet him?'

'You already did.'

She stood motionless.

'I see you did not realise it. I cannot help you there. We did our part and your internship is officially over.'

She protested, 'Please let me see him. After all, he sent me here, so why can't I see him?'

'I am sorry but that's not in my capacity. You would have seen him if you were meant to. I cannot alter that.'

She stood numb from the hurtful feeling of knowing that she had missed something critical. She did not know how that was to affect her but she felt very empty. That was like putting a scrumptious meal in front of a hungry man but taking away his sense of taste. What hurt her more than knowing that she could not see him again was the fact that she was not wise enough to realise when she had come across him!

'And by the way, you need to find your way out of here.'

'How do you mean? Won't Bhanudas escort me out?'

'No, as I said, your internship is over. And I would recommend you find your way out before you are stuck.'

Meera did not understand what he meant when he said 'before she was stuck', but she knew enough by now to not take his word lightly. 'But where should I go? How can I get out?'

'By proving that your purpose of this visit is accomplished. You need to find out how to do that on your own.'

She was flabbergasted at the way she was being treated but more than that, she was scared at the word 'stuck'. She was already in a strange land and she did not want to be at someone's mercy.

In a few moments, she was standing outside the castle but she had no idea where to go next.

Chapter NINETEEN
Back in the Train

The train wheels came to a halt with such a screeching sound that everyone opened their eyes in alarm. Meera looked out of the window to find that the train was standing somewhere in the wilderness. Inquiries were made and it was discovered that some villagers heedlessly crossing the track were saved in the nick of time. Meera thanked God quietly and expressed her anger about the careless people.

And then she realised that she was in a train. Trains picking up souls to a new destination! Where was she? She looked around with panic stricken face only to find familiar faces who fortunately didn't notice her. She turned her face away towards the window and tried to dig out the threads of what seemed fantastic like a dream and yet, detailed like reality. Thus, slowly she wove the fabric of the most surreal experience she had had so far. The warp and weft threads moved and the pattern emerged. She was used to summoning Krsna but this time he had summoned her. It was only towards the end that she realised that the pattern reached no end and the design was left incomplete. She had failed him and her mind felt trapped.

PART FOUR

Chapter TWENTY
Return of a friend

As it usually happens, the remnants of the bizarre experience slowly faded to the back of Meera's mind and life resumed its banal course. But whenever it managed to claim her attention, albeit not so often, she would feel chained to some obscure fences, her mind vying to break free. She missed having someone to confide in. Her fingers would begin drafting emails to Charu but it was hard to find words to describe the occult experience. For hours, she would stare in an attempt to decipher the meaning of anything that occurred in the strange City of Justice but she always ended up with more questions than answers.

****

With the weather change, Meera fell sick and was once again confined to her bed. It would have been an ordinary case of viral fever except that it did not go away even on the seventh day. Her condition was worsening.

That morning, she lay silent when her mother brought in an unexpected doctor.

'Thank God, you are here. Please see her and do something!' came a plea of panic from Amrita.

The doctor sat beside Meera and quickly went through the formalities. Meera was too drugged to notice a new doctor and kept lying till she heard his voice. He was asking Amrita, 'Please show me her current prescriptions.'

That sounded too familiar even in her soporific state. She managed to open her eyes and look at her attendant. The face was familiar too except that she couldn't place it - fair skin, silky brown hair and look of a cerebral scholar. And there was something out of place about the whole situation - the face in front of her was more mature and grown up than what she remembered; her mind went back to a young boy with brown eyes - those bright eyes that flickered when he spoke enthusiastically. Of course... Shimit. Her mouth opened to say something except that it was too dry to emit any sound. And at that moment, she realised that it had been ages since she had last seen him. The neighborhood boy from her memory had transformed into a grown up man.

He immediately gave her some water and smiled. Meera did not fail to notice those brown eyes still glimmered with the same light.

He spoke warmly - 'Meera, I am so glad to see you.' One often hears those words - usually from strangers and if one counted the years she had spent not seeing him, Shimit very much fell into the category of strangers. But the warmth with which those words were delivered made the past eighteen years of strangeness vanish in an instant. A soft murmur came out from her lips, 'Me too.'

With some effort, she had already managed to sit up against the headrest.

'You should not scare your mother like this.'

'If I were her, I would have already given up on myself by now,' she said with a weak smile.

He got busy with his medical duties and after some writing, took out a white pill for her. 'Take this, your fever needs to go first of all.'

She obediently gulped it down.

'And now go to sleep, it causes severe drowsiness.'

She wanted to revolt but her eyelids were no longer in her control.

Over the next two days, she recovered at a much faster pace.

One afternoon, Meera casually asked her mother, 'How did you know Shimit was visiting?'

'His mom mentioned *na*. He is a very good doctor, his medicines always work. He said he will come back to visit you soon, I suppose he is out of town.'

Meera smiled at Amrita's seal of approval. 'I was a bit shocked to see him after such a long time.'

'Yes, he doesn't visit that often. But you were great childhood friends even though you were fairly apart in age.'

'I know Mom, I haven't forgotten.'

'It was a tragedy what happened to his father. His mom never really recovered.'

'Yes, I heard about it when I was in New York. What had happened exactly?'

'Well, his father was in the Army as you remember. And he was visiting some place in the Northeast...I forget it now...somewhere in Arunanchal Pradesh, I think. Some resurgence broke out and he was captured by the militants. The Army even tried to rescue him but there was an accident and he got shot down in the rescue operation. Nandita went berserk I remember.'

'I can imagine.'

'And to top it all, Shimit decided to do his fellowship in the Army medical services that same summer. It is supposedly risky; you can be summoned to accompany the soldiers anytime on emergency. That totally threw her off balance for some time. '

'Oh,' Meera went silent. 'She didn't want him to go to the Army? Did she think that the Army was responsible for Shimit's Dad?'

'That's the thing, no one knows what actually happened. So she did blame a large part on the Army. Even if the shot wasn't fired by an Army person, their failed operation cost him his life.

Considering that he had served the Army all his life and they failed to protect him, I can't blame Nandita for how she felt.'

'That is so tragic. Poor Aunty. But poor Shimit too. I'm sure he suffered as much.'

'Yes, I'm sure. He is one hell of a boy. I don't know why he isn't married yet.'

Meera could not help laughing. 'You measure everything on the one scale, don't you? Every good person has to be married.'

Amrita was pleasantly surprised to see Meera joking about marriage - or for that matter, about anything. She laughed along too. '*Kya karein, hamare zamane me to yahi hota tha!*[37] I had several proposals lined up when your Dad's offer came in. And I was only twenty one.'

****

Two days later, Meera was sitting in the garden enjoying the merciful afternoon sun. It was that trailing period of winters when the sun reaches its optimal warmth in the afternoons - not a degree more, not a degree less. Layered in a thin shawl, she reclined back on a big cane arm-chair with the neglected novel covering her face from the direct sunlight. They say sunlight should always be taken on the back and the warmth from a fire on the chest. They forgot to say where to take the sunlight of an overhead sun though.

At that moment, Shimit came in through the front gate.

'Today I feel my medicines work after all,' he said with a smile as sunny as the day.

She lazily lifted her head to look at him. 'Yeah I would say that too because the only other explanation is that it was the effect of seeing someone after eighteen years that energised my immune system and I wouldn't want to believe that.' She smiled back.

She stretched her hand for a handshake as he came closer but he tilted his face and scrunched his eyes as if to say, really? Before

---

[37] What can I say, this is what happened when we were younger.

she could respond, he leaned in, opened his right arm elegantly and hugged her - she could feel she was still a kid for him, just as she was when she went to play with his cousins as a twelve year old. He was sixteen then. Despite the age gap, she always felt closer to him and ended up spending more time asking him questions than playing with the cousins. She was a curious girl and he was a genius - the combination was a natural one.

The hug had resurrected all that and many other warm memories.

'How's life? Enjoying your work?' asked Meera.

'Yes, I love my work.'

'I'm not surprised. And I know how good you are too.'

'How is your work? I expected ton of weird things from you, you better not disappoint me.'

She laughed. 'I did not let my house burn down as you had predicted. Nor did I cause any strikes in my college. You were right about some things though, like me not turning out normal. The rest, I guess you already know...'

He nodded. His understanding demeanor and calm countenance reminded her of the endless times she had sought his counselling as a child. The matters were much more trivial back then but his soothing presence made her feel that nothing was too complicated to share with him.

She continued, switching to a more sober tone, 'Right now I'm standing at a cross road in my life. I know where I'm *not* going but I hope I could know where I *am* going. People keep consoling me that it doesn't matter but it's funny to see how even their own eyes do not believe them.'

He sat down on the opposite chair. 'I know how hard it must be on you...I do pity you.'

Meera's expression changed and her brows creased together as she tried to interpret his words. 'Did he say pity?' she thought with anger trickling in her mind.

He continued with a straight face, 'I understand it changes everything, your life is going to be hell from now on. I really feel sorry. God could not have been crueler.'

'I don't need your pity,' she said in a voice soaked in an unmistakable fury.

He stood up with his hands casually tucked in his pockets. 'Oh come on, I didn't mean it that way. But you also know what a mess you are in. This is pretty much the end of your dreams. It's not about you personally, but no one can come back from a situation like this...obviously you know that.'

'What the hell are you talking about? Please don't tell me what I can or cannot do.'

'Listen, I understand.' Shimit's hands gestured in the air. The unsaid 'calm down' was as audible as his vocal arguments. 'I'm just saying that it's okay to be an optimist when we are consoling someone else but we need to be a realist and acknowledge the situation we are in. You know how our society is, you know the challenges we face.'

'Is he really saying all this or am I dreaming? I suppose I was mistaken about him. Everyone is the same,' thought an incredulous Meera. She stared harder without trying to hide any exasperation. If a vacuum could be more hollow, fire warmer or time reversible, it might have been possible, although remotely, that a person could look more indignant.

'Thank you for at least being honest,' she added, 'even if your thoughts are offensive to me. As far as the question of what can I do in such a situation is concerned, allow me to show it to you in the time to come.'

With that quiet but deep assault of words, she got up and started walking away towards the house.

'Hey kiddo!' called out Shimit in a different and jovial tone that surprised her. But it was the word he had used to address her that made her spin around. That's what he called her out of affection when they were younger.

'What are you laughing about?' she asked in a tone still as stern.

'I was just checking if the circumstances had softened the girl I knew,' he grinned.

Her eyebrows puckered in perturbation.

'There, I knew you wouldn't disappoint me. I would love for you to show me and this world how it's done.' He was now looking at her steadily in eyes and his intentions were gradually dawning upon her.

Her whole being screamed, 'Yes, I'm not afraid.'

It was like he had made her stand in front of a mirror and shown her the smoldering embers she kept hidden in her spirit. He had made her witness her own strength that lay latent and was only waiting for the right catalyst to soar. And, he had done it without preaching a single word or consoling.

'So as far as standing at a crossroads is concerned, these are the moments we live for. You have always been rational about things, so it would be uncharacteristic of you to change your course out of mere pressure or social risks. As a great poet has said-

"Tundi-e-baad-e-mukhalif se na ghabra, ae uqaab

Ye to chalti hai tujhe ooncha udaane ke liye"'

Her curious eyes glanced up at him and he smiled.

'*Uqaab* means an eagle. *Baad* is the wind and *tundi* means violent. The interesting word is *mukhalif* - it means in an opposite direction. Do not fear the violent winds blowing against you, my dear eagle. They blow merely to make you soar higher.'

She looked at him in admiration, in respect. She wanted to cry out, 'Where have you been all this while? I missed you so!' but settled with an acknowledging smile and humble eyes.

She collected herself and said, 'I'm sorry I misjudged you. How could I even think that you'd tear me down?'

'Nah. Everything is fine as long as you don't misjudge yourself. Never ever lose your spirit. I don't know how much you recollect, but when I look at you, I only remember a spirited and cheerful girl who never thought twice about the world, who lived life whole-heartedly. I would be devastated to see her give up.'

'I wish you had come earlier, maybe you could have helped avoid...'

He held her shoulders, 'Meera.'

Meera stopped.

'No one would have avoided anything, and what has happened has happened. Don't waste a single moment twisting and turning over it. Live now, enjoy now.'

She nodded and hugged him.

'Thanks.'

'Anytime, kiddo.'

As the sun swept farther away, they moved into the house.

It was time to catch up on the long past and Meera could see that Shimit deliberately tried to focus the conversation on her and get her to talk about her thoughts. With little encouragement, she even disclosed her present spiritual inclinations and inexplicable encounters with Krsna.

'Unfortunately, I'm no spiritual guru. But I think you are holding up great. I can already see a drastic change from the girl who fainted at the airport.'

Meera's eyebrows immediately shot up.

Shimit smiled and continued, 'Yeah, don't look so alarmed, your Mom told me about that. You have evolved and that's what matters.'

The conversation was briefly interrupted as she went in the kitchen to make tea.

'I see a lot of photos in here,' commented Shimit on the numerous frames hanging along the corridor and the walls.

Meera entered with a tray holding two cups of steaming hot tea. Her eyes lit up as she responded, 'Yeah, I took those.'

'Really? They are quite impressive. By the way, what's this?' he pointed to a big square photo frame and walked up to it. The photo he referred to showed a metallic bronzish jagged circle filled with darkness except for a rough smaller co-centric circle inside. The area outside the bigger circle seemed like a collage of colors.

'Is it like a *guess what* photography experiment?'

She chuckled. 'You can say that. It's the top view...or bottom view...of a bell that you see at the temples. I took this photo at a monastery by placing the camera directly under the bell. You wouldn't believe how ridiculously hard it can be to get the exact right angle and the bell to be absolutely stationary.' Her fingers moved to the colorful bits around the rim and she explained, 'Outside here, I just photoshopped numerous tiny faces, bodies and scenes from a lot of religious places I have visited in India. These are mostly the pictures taken of people right after they have rung the bell.'

'Wow, I didn't expect that much explanation behind this seemingly...um crazy...picture.' He leaned forward to look at the faces closely.

Meera's smile lingered while continuing to look at the picture - 'So, this monk at that monastery told me that ringing the bell helps to raise our consciousness and prepare ourselves to feel the God inside us. I became intrigued and started noticing whenever a person rang the bell at any temple and how his expressions varied during and after it. But I rarely saw anyone smiling afterwards. In fact, I saw them getting tense and then praying...which was very counter intuitive to me. I would think one would smile to prepare themselves to meet God...you know. So, the pictures here are different expressions I captured right after someone rang the bell.' She squinted and moved closer to the frame. 'See, I wish there were more smiling faces in here. Why be so serious when praying?'

Shimit stared at the picture for a few moments. He added, 'I would have thought it's like a doorbell...you know. You ring a bell when you are visiting someone, so why not do it with God too?'

'That's interesting. I never thought it like that. But Muslims and Christians have no bells at the mosques and churches...does it mean they just crash in?'

He chuckled. 'Well. Here's a thought on why there should be no bells - we don't ring bells when we are entering our homes, we don't need to alert anyone. I suppose our Hindu Gods are more formal and want their children to announce when they are coming,' he added teasingly.

Her focus was broken as she thought over his simple but acute reply. 'That's a witty one,' she admitted.

She walked away while he continued watching the faces in the picture. 'You know, you should do an exhibition of your photographs.'

'Yeah, right, right. I don't know what I'm doing. I haven't printed my photographs in a long time now.'

Suddenly, she left the room and returned with a big bag in her hand. She opened it and took out her camera carefully.

'Let me see,' asked Shimit with a stretched hand.

She handed the camera to him.

He fidgeted with the buttons and started seeing her photographs. 'Not bad.'

'Thank you.'

'I meant the camera.'

Both of them smiled.

'It's a bit old though now, isn't it?' He raised it to his eyes and pointed the lens towards her.

'Yeah, I have had it for few years now. Still, it's the second most expensive item I own. I have an emotional attachment to it, I guess.'

He clicked a few shots before handing it back to her. She took on her favorite position behind the eyepiece and said, 'Let me click some profile pictures for you. May be you can commission me when you win a Nobel Prize or something.'

He laughed, 'Pulling my leg, huh?'

'Not at all Mr. AIIMS. Don't think that I'm unaware of your professional accomplishments. Mom always told me when you were featured in newspapers. Meera, do you know Shimit received a Gold Medal at AIIMS? Do you know I saw him in an article on Hindu today? Shimit was featured in an article about some complicated surgery blah blah blah. I was like please, give me a break. Does this guy have nothing better to do than work?'

He kept laughing, 'Yeah the sad guy who is happiest amongst sick bodies.'

He didn't have to pose as Meera clicked a stream of shots before letting him off the hook. 'Done,' she said as she put down the camera.

'Already?'

'Yes. I don't do those passport type photos you know. But whenever you are in the mood, we can do a professional shoot too.'

'And since when did you become a professional photographer?'

'Oh well, I am not professional but you can't tell from my photos. Really, I'll get you some good pictures.'

'Oh no, I'm not interested in my photo shoot, but I think you should pursue this professionally. Your body is exuding passion right now and if you like something that much, you might as well make some money from it.'

'I don't know...I never pursued my interests seriously. But then, I had a job to worry about.'

'Right. What are you doing now?'

'That's the thing. I was thinking about taking on a job. Mom and Dad were worried about me till now, they were not sure if working was a good idea in my condition. I don't know but I feel extremely anxious sometimes and it's not always about my divorce. I think I'm growing restless because I don't have a job anymore. I never imagined sitting idle like this. So, I feel I should start working.'

'You don't sound very excited going back to your job though.'

'Yeah, it will be good that I'll go out and start mingling with people but frankly, I don't feel the ambition or enthusiasm I had earlier. I mean, it's just a job for me now. I was good and I'll hopefully land a good job soon. In fact, some of my friends have already applied on my behalf at various places.'

'Actually you diagnosed your problem correctly. That anxiousness you mentioned is not so much about not earning as it is about lack of accomplishment.'

'Hm...I'm listening.'

'We are human and until we can measure our success and our achievement, the fulfillment doesn't come. I know you are trying your spiritual zen and what not, but you can't directly jump there, you have to make intermediate stops. You can't wean off drugs directly, you need a substitute first. Till you get to the point where you are permanently at zen, you need to feel stronger and confident - and that comes from accomplishing something.'

He added, 'And that's the thing. This accomplishment does not have to come from a job or paycheck, but it has to be something tangible or material that your senses can feel. That feeling is what happiness is really about. Sometimes, it comes from a fulfilling relationship, sometimes from a fulfilling line of work, sometimes from charity but you need to have it. Remember, I'm talking about non-trivial accomplishments - not a title or promotion per se. Maybe cooking a delicious meal for a friend serves that purpose for someone,' he said taking a low bow, adding, 'and may be composing a serene tune for his kid does that for a famous composer - it's about being appreciated. Everyone, I repeat - everyone, wants to be appreciated.'

She nodded.

He continued, 'I know this from myself. I have done 48 hours of continuous duty many a times during my medical studies, but what made me really tired was when a month passed by without a challenging case that I could successfully handle. That's called an itch for accomplishment and every talented person has it. I know I sound like a big douchebag patronising myself right now, but what I'm telling you is exactly what you need. Only accomplishment and appreciation can give you the peace you need to continue on your spiritual path. Make yourself feel accomplished again.'

She knew he was right. He let his words echo in her mind - Make yourself feel accomplished again.

****

'How did you like New York?'

'Loved it. In fact...' she got up abruptly and went up to her room. For a minute or two, she kept rummaging through her drawer. Then, she turned around with a diary in her hand. She turned the pages till she found what she was looking for. 'You like poetry, no?'

'Oh yes.'

'Here, that's my first impression of New York,' she said while handing it over to him.

A faint smile came to his lips as he read it.

There was the earth engulfing those men and women,
As they vanished down from the roads
And then I see, Oh! it's the subway

The night isn't dark here, and the city doesn't sleep
Dazzled in the light, I am wondering where I am
And then I notice, Oh! it's Times Square

2 am and the train is full,
I look into the anxious faces around
Some aware of their existence and many, not

A massive trench cuts out in the heart of city
What is left makes me imagine that which is no more
The strange emptiness in the air may make you shiver
And you will see that it's Ground Zero

Suddenly you'll find people rushing past,
For no reason that you can physically see
They whisper, blink and express with everything but words
Don't worry, it's the famous Wall Street

Standing on Jersey waterfront, I see the magnificent skyline
A greenish copper lady standing to my right
Is it the shine of stars or the man-made wonders?
When I feel accompanied in the solitude and look for solitude in the
crowd
And then I smile- It's New York.

'It's stupid and childish I know, but that's how I felt when I first experienced it,' she said.

'No, it's great, I love it!'

He flipped the pages and opened an earlier one.

'Another poem! Let me read this one.'

The weather is colder
My phone is not ringing
The park benches are untaken
The sidewalk is lonely
The breeze has lost its sweetness
The trees look eerie
Crowd is daunting
Coffee shops don't look inviting
Clock hands move slowly
Movies are not charming
New York is empty
Without You

'Very romantic! I didn't know you could wield a pen that well,' he started but stopped after seeing Meera looking far away.

Her features softened, 'It was for my husband.'

He closed his eyes in regret, 'I'm sorry.'

'No, no, don't worry. I'm okay.'

'Remember the good times, it helps. Don't punish yourself for the bad ones, you couldn't have controlled it.'

'But it haunts sometimes. Time has a nature of drifting and bringing up its torments of the past.'

'I understand what you mean.'

A noticeable pause followed while a silent understanding was exchanged.

'Bad divorce, *na*?'

'Gut wrenching.'

'You wanted the divorce, I hope? I mean I hope it's happening as per your consent.'

She nodded. 'You know there was a time when I felt I could conquer anything. I believed in goodness, beautiful things. I thought things are black and white...good or bad...and that I can make things alright. As life moved on, you happened to realise it's not black and white...its grey. It's not just good or bad, right or wrong...it's so...'

'Complicated?'

She turned to look at him. 'Yes. It's so complicated. You could try but you really can't change it. I wish people introspected before getting into relationships...figure out their priorities, you know? Figure out what matters a lot to them and then make sure it's there in the other person. Else you can never be happy in the long run.'

'What happened really?'

'Dream transformed into a nightmare. Like when you are chasing girls on a bike, it's fun you know. Like going to a cool cafe again and again to order a dessert that made your girlfriend laugh last time...that is fun even when you are short on cash and you are spending your canteen budget on an expensive date...even when you don't know anything is going to happen. All that is fun. And then you focus on getting a 'yes' when you propose. That is fun. And then you focus on how to get her family to say 'yes'...at least in India. That is also interesting to you, it keeps you focused on a result. Once you get that, you talk about the wedding ceremony and honeymoon and all that bullshit. That again is fun...laughter you know. Then, all of a sudden, you are married and you have no more targets. Not all marriages are like that but let's say some, some unfortunate ones are. You are not on a mission...leave apart a fun one at that...anymore. You are a regular guy with a regular life with regular responsibilities. And you build these fantastic expectations. But there's no fun in that.'

She smiled in derision. 'And then, one of them starts dying inside. Maybe the other one is dying too but they don't even bother to die together...'

'I don't know if I should ask, but do you still love him?'

She shook her head in negative in a slow motion. 'There was no he left, there was no I left. We were just apparitions of our real selves forced to live under a roof. One day, I thought I'd end the misery...but I couldn't...I still had some debt of life left to repay. I still thought I could weather it. I came back hoping to live but it was tough in the beginning. It seemed like people wanted me to cry and be sorry for myself. They wanted my eyes to not forget the pain. My merits somehow didn't count anymore...my accomplishments didn't matter. I was not good enough for a guy, so what can I be good enough for?...But soon I realised they never mattered. What matters is what I think of myself.'

****

Shimit got up to leave after realising he had been out for longer than he had expected. A doctor's dutiful message followed about sticking to the prescribed medications and instructions. And then he resorted to something more non-customary.

'I would like to invite you and your parents for a home cooked dinner, I'm sure it would be good for Mom to have some guests too.'

'Oh, I would love to come. Dad is out these days as you know, but Ma and I'll come. But let's order something, no? I would really not want to trouble aunty.'

'Well, it won't be the aunty who is cooking, so don't worry.'

Meera's eyebrows went up, 'Who's cooking then?'

'I am.'

'Oh. Really? Awesome.'

He laughed, 'I love cooking, don't worry.'

'I can't wait to see how you cook.'

'I always like to have new people to experiment upon. So, thank you,' he smiled playfully. 'Tomorrow night, don't forget!'

Meera cleaned up the kitchen while thinking about her conversation with Shimit. Cleaning always helped her organise her thoughts. The more she thought about their childhood days, the happier she got. But nothing compared to the realisation that he still possessed that magic effect - the one he had used to make her discover herself. It was like he carried stardust with him and she would be revealed in new forms whenever their paths crossed. Her thoughts also wandered to the little she knew about his personal tragedies from her mother. Despite all the ghastly things he had gone through, he showed no bitterness or regrets.

She neatly arranged the tea cups on the shelf and stacked the sugar and tea-leaves jars. Her appraising glance swept the kitchen platform - 'Yes, everything looks perfect,' she thought, 'and nice.' She was in simple words, happy.

Amrita came in just then and made a big fuss over seeing Meera out of her bed. She touched her forehead and finally calmed down upon finding no signs of fever. Meera informed her of Shimit's invitation.

'Yeah, I remember Nandita mentioned he loves cooking. In fact, he nearly sent off their cooking maid last time when he was visiting and insisted on cooking for her himself.'

****

As soon as the iron-gate creaked open, a horde of memories came gushing back to Meera about the garden and the house. She and Amrita had not even reached the front door when Shimit came out to receive them. He hugged them both and led their way inside. The house screamed of its Army roots and simplicity. Not a single item lay astray or unorganised. The soothing wooden accents and blinds elegantly gave the white walls a rich feel. Everything looked the same as she remembered it, except a garland on Shimit's Dad's photo.

Meera's eyes welled up on seeing his Mom; part in grief and part in admiration. Her movements were restricted due to a paralysis attack and her frailer body betrayed the burden of her torment. But the eyes still shone of that old pride and dignity; she was still as much an Army man's wife as she could be. She hugged Meera warmly yet strongly, whispering her blessings. Meera could see where Shimit got his relentless energy and knack to spread around his own strength from. After exchanging pleasantries, she went in the kitchen to hand over what she had brought.

The kitchen had been refurbished with modern amenities. A wide smile crept up to her face on seeing Shimit chopping onions wearing a clean white apron.

'What's in the box?' he asked looking at her while his fingers still continued.

'Careful,' she warned.

He just smiled. He appeared to be at same ease on the chopping board as he would be in an operating room.

'Its *ras malai*, I hope aunty likes it.'

'Oh nice! Yes, she loves it. And I know she will love it more coming from Amrita aunty.'

'Oh.'

He looked at her quizzically.

'Mom did not make it, I did.'

He raised his eyebrows in a manner indicating he was impressed. She added, 'Under Mom's instructions though, so I hope it won't be a disappointment.'

He had finished chopping, so he turned around to face her. 'I'm sure she'll love it.'

She smiled.

For the next hour, she watched him unleash his cooking skills to the maximum effect. The way he minced the garlic with the broad surface of the knife in a flawless press, the way he put cumin seeds at the precise temperature of the oil, the way he added a sprig of coriander and mint leaves to enhance the green color while grinding spinach - it was like an artist giving a live perfected performance. After chit-chatting initially, she had just gone silent to relish the demonstration without any distractions. Slowly the appetizing aromas began making her hungrier than she thought was possible.

Shimit bent to take out the vessel from the oven as the alarm went off. The pot was covered with a layer of damp flour upon seeing which Meera broke her silence, 'Biryani?'

'Yeah, you like it?'

'Oh, you have no idea!' she grinned.

He added the freshest looking *paneer* she had ever seen to the most appetizing green looking spinach gravy and poured a little bit of cream before turning the burner off. The last step was to prepare the *tadka* and a sizzling sound went off as he sprinkled the chillies and seeds on the hot ghee. Before any spices burned, he had deftly dipped the ladle in the pot of *dal* covering the lid instantaneously. He washed his hands and slid the apron off his head. The performance was over and the good part was that the actual outcome of it was still left to be consumed. Meera helped him carry the serving dishes to the previously laid-out table.

Shimit went in the sitting room and had casually struck a conversation in the middle of which he made Nandita get up with his help. He then chatted and laughed with Nandita and Amrita while inconspicuously walking her to the dining table. Meera just observed in awe and respect - he had made Nandita walk to the table with his support, without making it evident that he was doing so. And the theme reiterated itself throughout the night as he took care of her needs without a single display of offending servility. Nandita paid full attention to him and made up for her absence in the kitchen by catering to his likes and dislikes on the table. She knew exactly when to offer him more.

The unsaid understanding between them had made a deep impression on Meera's being as her heart asked herself - 'Why do we forget to appreciate the simplest things in life? Why do we lose what we have for what we don't? No one steals our happiness from us but ourselves.' She felt she had a lot to be thankful for that she kept ignoring. She silently thanked God for all the things she still had.

The simple yet heavenly dinner - dal, palak paneer, roti, salad and biryani - was followed by Meera's dessert. Her efforts were generously appreciated and no one minded her penurious use of the sugar. She anxiously glanced at Shimit as he took his first portion. He betrayed no expression but the way he finished it quickly before going for a second helping gave her some relief.

After helping Shimit clear up the table, she prepared coffee for everyone. Leaving their mothers to their domestic topics, they strolled out in the garden.

'You seem lost, didn't like the food?' his voice recaptured her attention.

'Not at all...I don't remember the last time I ate so much!'

'By the way Meera, you should cook more often.'

She didn't know why but that made her very happy. His approval always mattered but she found no voice to thank him.

'How long is your vacation?'

'Two more weeks. I have come after such a long time that I have lot of holidays left. Actually...'

She saw an unusual display of emotion on his face. 'What?'

'I don't like coming for fewer days and leaving Mom again and again. I prefer longer vacations so that I can spend more quality time with her.'

She nodded, she understood perfectly what he meant. She felt the same whenever she visited from the USA. 'I heard about Uncle when I was in New York. I wanted to even reach out to you but couldn't figure what I would say. I still regret not calling you then.'

His face convulsed in pain for a flash before he regained his composure. 'I understand, take it easy. I mean, Mom had it harder. If he had died in a war, it might have been easier to accept, but it was just unfortunate that he happened to be there when the tribal insurgents attacked.'

Silence followed.

He continued, 'Dad knew what being in Army entailed. I did too. Actually Mom does too but it's a different thing to know and to live through it. She had a very tough time accepting it.'

'Did that make you go to the Army Medical Services?' she asked flat out.

He nodded. 'I knew how much respect Dad had for his duty. I thought this would be my tribute to him.'

'You should have taken your Mom's permission though. She had already suffered enough, perhaps you could have relieved her of more pain...you know. I mean I know what you are saying but at the same time, it might not be fair on her.' Meera was surprised by the conviction and authority in her voice on someone else's matter. Usually she never judged, but she was close to Shimit's family and wanted to talk to him in the hope of sharing his hidden grief or whatever.

'Why do you think I didn't take her permission? I gave her the complete choice and she did not stop me even once. That's when I knew she cared as much for Dad's principles but her maternal instincts were prohibiting her from accepting it. She thought something unfortunate might happen to me too. But I know that if she stopped me from going, she would regret it later. I could never inflict an incurable regret on her. Only pride could heal her, I am trying to make her proud and she will be one day.'

Meera looked at him as he stared afar. No, there was no pain, he was at utter peace with his life and his clarity of thoughts reflected in a determined face devoid of frowns. He and his Mom were not the ones who needed help.

'I wish I could be this way,' she thought. And then, she smiled at her own thought. Every encounter with Shimit ended with the same feeling - I wish I could be like him.

Then she remembered another thing she needed to discuss with him.

'I heard back from a friend in California. He had applied to a very lucrative opening on my behalf and I interviewed for it last week. They got back to him only today. They want to extend an offer to me and he thinks it's going to be better than we expected before. In short, it's the perfect offer I could ever get.'

'Do you want to go back to the USA?'

'I don't know...' her voice trailed off. She added, 'But, then I feel why not? This is the best I'm going to get. And I'm good at it.'

'What you can do and what you want to do are two different things.'

'How do you mean?'

'I mean that you have always been a consultant and it's easy for you to work in that role. It's familiar and you are good at it. You will, I'm sure, get jobs easily. But you should ask if that is what you really want.'

She laughed. 'Well, I would really want to be a photographer, but you know that's probably not happening now.'

'Why not? Who is stopping you?'

She wanted to say 'I have no background' or 'I am not formally trained for it' or 'who would hire me?' before she thought about it herself and found the answers surprisingly simple. She murmured, 'No one is stopping me.'

'We always find a way to do what we really want. So, if this is what you want, make yourself find that path.'

'I don't know...' She knew he was right but her circumstances made her feel weak. 'Perhaps this job will give me that feeling of accomplishment we talked about.'

'That is something only you can know. Will it?'

She stayed silent.

He added, 'If you think its fine, I would like to take you to a place tomorrow.'

'What place?'

'A place where I sometimes find my answers.'

'Sounds like a spiritual odyssey.'

He laughed, 'No, nothing like that. As I said, I'm no spiritual expert. But it worked for me and it might work for you. No obligation, though.'

'No, I would like to see it too. If it helped you, I can't think of a better place to try.'

'You use superlatives a lot,' he said in a dismissive but kind tone.

She wanted to say 'not for everyone' but refrained.

****

Meera closed the book in frustration. She had been trying to concentrate but had not even advanced two pages in the last hour. Her thoughts kept wandering to the dinner, more specifically to Shimit and his Mom. Sometimes, we think that we are the lone bearer of misfortunes, the personal custodian of tragedies until we come across those who are not only hit by worse things but choose to endure it with dignity. Meera reflected how she alone was to be blamed for magnifying her disadvantages and undermining her strengths. Life is bigger than any problem - we only need to look beyond it.

Each contemplation made her feel more and more respectful towards Shimit. He was not someone who just preached, he had the courage to put it in action. In life's decisive moments, he stood tall and dignified. Her mind kept replaying the reel of Shimit Tagore on loop. 'He is such an awesome guy, I hope he gets every happiness in this world,' was the last thought before her eyes surrendered to sleep.

Chapter TWENTY-ONE
Five: Conversation of Heart

It was early afternoon when Shimit came to pick Meera up in his gypsy for their proposed trip and refused to divulge any details about where they were going.

'Okay, if we are going for this, you have to trust me throughout this thing. No questions allowed and don't let any doubt creep in. Do you trust me?'

She did not know what she was committing to but she had only one answer for his question.

'Fine. But what exactly is going to be my question? I mean, what am I going to ask?' she asked nervously.

'It's your question, so you should know. And decide that before we leave because if you don't know the question, all answers will be equally wrong.'

She nodded. She reflected until she knew what she was going to ask. 'Ok, I know now. Let's go.'

They drove north until the mountains came closer and the jungle began.

'Wow, looks very scenic. Why didn't you tell me earlier? I would have brought my camera!'

He said nothing as if she didn't even exist. This ruffled her a bit and she tried to provoke him into speaking, without success. She finally gave up.

After some time, he turned into a lane that went inside the jungle and stopped in front of a gate that said 'private property'.

He got out and talked to the watchman for a couple of minutes. The watchman handed him something and opened the door obediently. They drove in and past the main house until they came to a big garage-like structure standing in the middle of a huge ground. It was made of old wood and the paint was chipping away at multiple places.

'This is it. Come on in,' said Shimit while turning off the engine and jumping out as Meera curiously followed. He took out a key from his pocket and turned open the lock.

She went in to examine. The barn was mostly empty except for some haystacks in the corner. 'What is so special about this place?' she thought.

'Meera!' he called in a commanding voice while staying at the door.

'What?'

'This is where you will find your answers and until you do, I will not let you out.'

Her face suddenly looked alarmed - 'What the fuck is he talking about?'

'Just look for the answers and they will come. Good luck. Don't be scared, you will thank me later.'

And saying that, he went out, locking the door after him.

****

She ran like crazy to the door and shouted out, 'What the hell are you doing, Shimit? I don't like such jokes! Get me out.'

No sound.

She repeated ten and then twenty times but no voice or footstep came back. She banged on the door with angry fists and her foot. Her hands immediately shot to her pocket but she realised he had borrowed her cell phone earlier and not returned it. She was seething in anger now and kept seething until the fury cooled down on its own.

For the first time, she paid attention to the pin drop silence and vast emptiness of the barn. 'This is not cool,' came an anxious voice from her mind.

Nervously, she surveyed the ground and walls. It was made up of wide planks of wood with uneven gaps and holes in between that let in golden lines of sunrays - the only light source in an otherwise dark shed. The bright afternoon ensured that there was ample amount of light inside which she was extremely thankful for. But soon the sun would start to set and the darkness would creep in faster, especially since they were somewhere in the mountains. Meera tried to brush the discomforting fact aside - 'Shimit can't be that insane.'

As minutes passed by and her initial anxiety subsided, she thought about everything he had said. He knew she would be scared and had tried to reassure her. Besides, she had herself given him the word that she trusted him and this was the chance to prove it. Since no sound had come from the gypsy, she was confident that he had not left the premises. She shouted again to an imaginary Shimit, whom she believed was sitting outside - 'Fine, I get it. You are trying to scare me, but I don't know how that is going to give me my answers!'

She thought - 'Come on Meera, you can do better than that. Now that you have decided to trust him, try to understand what he is doing. What purpose is solved by leaving you alone in this forsaken barn where not even a single window exists? Either this is a bewitched place and some miracle will unfold when you will ask the right question or there is some secret answer lying here that you need to uncover.' She quickly brushed aside both the possibilities. 'No, Shimit is more sensible than that.'

She had checked out the barn carefully but found nothing of interest. It was a damned old creaky empty place and she was alone, absolutely alone. She strolled and sat down on the hay. Faint sounds of chirping birds floated over from outside, interrupted only by the gentle rustle of leaves. It was a weird feeling being captured in a restrained space when nature seemed so close outside. She wanted to look at the beauty of the mountains and the jungle but here she was in this weird scary room...

'Maybe you are missing the most obvious thing. What is obvious about this barn?'

She looked and looked.

'It is huge and it is empty.' Also, old and smelly but she doubted that could have any connection with Shimit's mystery.

'It is empty and the only person in here is you. Assuming Shimit is a rational guy who doesn't believe in supernatural things, that means that the only person who can give the answer is you.'

'Ah. Now, that sounds more promising and philosophical. But if I had the answer, I would have already got it, no? This is getting me nowhere.'

'Maybe you never asked!'

'Ok, I'll ask now - Meera, should you take that job in California?'

She breathed slower as she tried to concentrate. No, no answer came. She got up impatiently and changed her position. She repeated the question but to no avail. The wind outside was now billowing more prominently and the birds apparently had flown away. She walked to the door and bent down to look outside but the gap was not wide enough to show anything meaningful. She started walking around, dejected. She was no longer aware of the dimming light, the precariousness of the situation, the vacuousness of the surrounding or the melancholy in the air.

After more futile attempts, she sunk to the floor in the middle of the shed and closed her eyes. Strangely, she was no more thinking of escaping. The only thing that occupied her mind was how to find her answer. Even she did not want to get out of this place before finding it. 'Maybe Krsna will help me'.

'Krsna, are you there?'

The idols of Banke Bihari and the other temples came up but the visions of her own Krsna denied her.

'Ok, let's try it differently.' She opened her mouth and said out loud, 'Yes, I'm going to USA and taking up that job. It's decided!'

She immediately felt dejected and felt her heart crying out, "No! I don't want to. I came back for a reason and I am not going back! I don't care about your stupid job!"

And, then began her self-interrogation with her heart.

She asked herself loudly, 'Then, what do you want?'

She again listened to her heart and the answer came in quietly through her inner voice. Her heart was telling her, "Why don't you consider photography? At least, give it a try! I deserve a chance!"

Meera replied to her heart out loud, 'Of course, you deserve every chance but how will it work? I don't know anything about it.'

But her heart wasn't going to give up so easily. It retorted through her thoughts – "You know everything about how photographs are taken, don't lie!"

'Okay, okay but it's different doing it for pleasure and doing it professionally. Please understand.'

"All I care for is happiness. It is your job to figure out the rest. I only tell you where the happiness lies."

Meera held her temples in her fingers. She realised she had just witnessed a live argument between her mind and her heart. Her heart had given her the answer and that too so clearly. If only she'd always listened to it. Yes, don't suppress your heart, let it express itself. We often fail to take heed in the name of rationality but there exists no better litmus test for happiness - your heart will always tell you when you are happy and when you are not.

She could barely believe any of it. Still, it was less incredulous than talking to Krsna, she thought.

****

She gently got up and walked to the door.

'Shimit, I have found my answer!' she said in a loud voice. She doubted no more whether or not he was standing outside. She knew his trick had worked and that he knew it would work.

'What a devil you are!' was her first sentence as he opened the door.

He did not have any mischievous smile on his lips - just a subtle pride on having his confidence in her rewarded.

'I knew you would find it and you did a good job. It took me longer than this to find out mine.'

She stared at him. 'How did you know it would work?'

'When we are pushed to the edge and left with no choice, we usually find our answers on our own. It's impossible to find them externally anyway but we often don't have the courage to look inside. Since you have been spending time alone already, I was more confident that you would find it sooner. Normally, people are scared to spend time with themselves because they are afraid to scratch the surface. If they start introspecting - who knows what unresolved issues may lie within? It takes more courage to look within than outside.'

She thought about the bungee jump and how that leap of faith had helped her make up her mind about the divorce. Yes, when we are on the edge, the answers come - she thought.

He continued, 'By forcing you to be confined in a physical space with no distractions, it created an ideal environment for you to communicate with yourself. And once that happens, everything becomes clear. The details may vary from person to person but the outline remains the same - you excavate your answer from yourself.

I truly believe that our mind knows all the answers - not just to our personal questions but to everything. It is just a matter of helping the revelation.'

Meera laughed. 'Did you say you had no interest in spirituality? What do you think this whole revelation is? To shut yourself to discover yourself - is it different than meditation? Shimit, you have no clue of how high a spiritual plane you live on. If this is not spirituality, I don't know what is. As you said, your mind has not yet been made aware of your spiritual nature.'

Shimit stared at her.

She continued, 'And the funny thing is I thought I was spiritual. I am but I could not have thought of such an ingenious technique to interrogate myself.'

He smiled, 'So I came to teach you something and ended up being taught myself?'

'Let's just say we were destined to come here to help each other reveal ourselves.'

She suddenly felt awfully close to him.

****

The evening was well under way but Shimit raced the gypsy adroitly along the sinuous roads to beat the approaching darkness.

'How did you discover that barn? Whose is it?' Meera could no longer contain her endless list of questions.

'A friend who helped me find my answer. Since then I have come here a couple of times when I needed it. You are the first person I've taken there though.'

Once they crossed the mountain, they halted at a small roadside *dhaba* for the much needed chai break. He brought two small glasses of steaming hot tea and handed one to Meera who had found her way to sit on top of the bonnet. Her eyes were fireflies. She smiled at him and he smiled back as they continued sipping the tea peacefully.

'Life's a bitch at times, isn't it?' he said unexpectedly.

She stared at him in surprise. It was not a sentence she could associate with him. He was lost in his thoughts as she replied, 'I am usually the one saying that but I try not to anymore.'

'Yeah, I'm saying it on our behalf. And I know both of us are not going to give up on life.'

She continued looking at him in anticipation. He seemed to be lugging some weight on his shoulders and she wanted to help him. She didn't know if she could but she would try everything to be able to.

After few minutes of brainstorming, he shook his head vigorously as if exorcising the negative thoughts that had dared to come to him.

He donned a wide smile as he looked back at her, 'Never mind.'

He took their empty glasses and went back inside to return them. But Meera was not smiling anymore.

They resumed their journey quietly.

'What did you come to ask when your friend took you to that barn?'

He laughed. 'Take a guess.'

'Whether to join the Army fellowship program?'

His expression had changed as he nodded.

'Hm...I can imagine, must have been a tough call.'

He laughed again, 'You have no idea...'

She looked back at him and knew that his careless smile hid something painful. This time, he did answer back.

'I was about to propose to this girl when everything happened. My joining the Army not only meant tormenting Mom, but also giving my love up.'

Meera froze, not gradually like a lake but instantly like a raindrop. An 'Oh!' escaped from her mouth - hiding the deep wells of her dismay in its short sound. 'Shimit loved someone' kept echoing in her mind and pricking it. To make it worse, if that was possible, she didn't know why she should feel so. It was all too sudden and all too brutal like a fall from a sky-high building on to the tough concrete - a fall that not only breaks the body but the spirit if left alive. It's even hard to decide whether surviving it is a fortune or the biggest misery in itself. She gently turned her face away towards the window.

When she slowly glanced back at him after don't-know-how-long, he was focused on the road and had not noticed her silence. She pushed back her upheaval and tried to be normal again for his sake. This was her chance to be the friend he had always been to her.

'She didn't want you to join the fellowship either?'

'Nah. She wouldn't have minded it but I never disclosed my feelings to her since I had decided to join the program anyway.'

'What! You didn't disclose what you felt for her?'

He turned towards her to reveal his puckered brows. He had opened his mouth to say something but decided against it. In an instant, he had turned back to the road, his brows still clouded and that was the only hint of an inner turmoil that he would ever give out on the topic.

'Do you know what being in this program means?' he said after a long pause in a voice slightly sterner this time.

'I'm sorry I must not judge but please tell me there is a good reason for what you did.'

'I have an obligation to serve the Army whenever called upon during the fellowship.'

'And afterwards?'

'After that, it is up to me if I want to enter the Army formally or not. There's a bond if I leave the Army service but that's not the real issue. I most probably will continue with the Army. Army doctors serve on the warfront and in every aspect of the Army. I didn't want to impose an Army life on her.'

Meera winced upon the mention of the nameless friend. She was feeling too chagrined to know anything more about her and especially Shimit's attachment for her. But the call of friendship prevailed once again.

'Did she feel the same for you?' she asked in a trembling voice that, to her relief, went unnoticed by him.

'I don't know for sure but I think she would have accepted had I proposed. Anyway, doesn't matter now.'

Her fingers clenched the door handle tightly. It was taking her all her might to continue with this conversation.

'Shouldn't you have let her make that call?'

'No!'

'Why?'

'She might have still said yes.'

Meera closed her eyes in anguish and frustration. Despite everything, a strong feeling of empathy for that girl surged inside her.

'This is not fair to her, you know.'

'I wouldn't want anyone to be in that state that I have seen my Mom in. I don't want to discuss that. I know what it's like. And it is probably better for her to be treated unfairly in this manner than live through the consequences of my whim. I know what you are saying, I really do. I have utmost respect and love for her. But I know we had no commitments or even an inkling of each other's feelings, so I knew she would eventually move on.'

'And, did she move on?'

'I don't know, I did not keep in touch with her.'

Meera did not know how long it took to get back home. Any further questions were brushed aside by Shimit and to be fair, she had not insisted on knowing too much. She just felt like being left alone and understanding what was going in her mind...or heart. And until she knew that, she could not help him even if she wanted.

He had completely moved past the topic as he dropped her at her place.

She thanked him and genuinely at that - 'There are no words good enough or tone humble enough to thank you for making me go through that revelation.'

'Don't ruin it, kiddo,' he said getting back to his caring self. He added, 'There are two tragedies in life - one is not to get your heart's desire.' He paused meaningfully.

'And the other?' she asked on the cue.

'The other is to get it.'

She smiled.

'I didn't say it. Bernard Shaw did, so blame him.'

She knew she had to ask him one more question before she lost her courage - 'Do you still love her?'

His face showed a clear expression of surprise as if he wondered if the answer was not obvious, 'Of course and I always will.'

'I'm sorry. So, you will never move on?'

'Don't be. What does move on mean? Marry? How does that matter?'

'Sorry, I'm not getting it. You are just going to be sad for the rest of your life thinking of her, loving her and never...yeah never marrying or loving anyone else?'

He laughed and she did not know if she felt angry or stupid.

'I will always be *happy* thinking about her and loving her. I don't need to be with her or see her to love her. In fact, it doesn't even matter if she loved me or not because it wouldn't alter my feelings for her. And I still love life and would live it to the fullest. If things align in such a way, I would marry the right person too. Nothing can conflict with the way I feel for her. Why should it?'

A moment of silence ensued - Meera in a state of awe and Shimit in a state of veneration - his love was his act of praying.

'Thanks for listening to my chatter. It felt good to share it with someone,' said Shimit as he reversed the Gypsy.

As if nothing more was to be said or could be said, they departed with an unsaid valediction.

Meera kept standing and looking at the vanishing tail-lights.

Chapter TWENTY-TWO

Confessions

When she did go inside, she made an excuse to skip dinner and succinctly replied to Amrita's questions before retiring early to her room. She pushed the terrace door in her room wide open and stepped out in the night. The slight chill in the air felt like a welcome reminder of things that make us uncomfortable - including the feelings we deny. She was organising her reactions to Shimit's story and the pattern emerged clearly - he had comforted and helped her in the ways only a true friend can, she had unquestionable respect for him and she found it tough to bear that he had feelings for someone else. Someone *else* - yes, that was the key word because it means she wanted him to have feelings for her? And, that meant only one thing - she had feelings for him.

She shut her eyes as the inevitable thought surfaced and flaunted itself in front of her. She knew it and somehow, thought that she could deny it. For so many days, she had thought of no one but him and his conversations. She realised that she respected him to that degree where reverence transformed into deeper feelings. Yes, there was no scope of any more denial about how she felt for Shimit. And she felt it as deeply as there is darkness in the shadow.

But the realisation was also like a fresh wound that would take time to get used to. For now she just felt fragile because she was not prepared to have feelings for a person again - at least, not yet. She had seen how love blossomed before and she was equally well aware of how fast it had withered. She had survived it once but twice was beyond her capacity. Besides, this was a straight case of one-sided feelings with its own twists and tragedies. She wasn't sure what made her feel worse - that it would remain one sided or that she was venturing into the dangerous territory of matters of the heart.

Then, she laughed - silently - at her own irony. The day she discovered her feelings was the day she was made aware that her feelings couldn't amount to anything. Her object of affection had affection for another object - she thought amusingly.

'You and your sense of humour,' she said looking at the sky.

It tired her to even think any more of it. And that helplessness made her feel very close to her favorite literary character and someone with a personality starkly polar to hers - Scarlett O'Hara. She merely uttered, 'I'll think about it tomorrow.'

****

It was hard to face Shimit and act normally until she had accepted her feelings and become comfortable with them. Not that she wanted anything from him, but she did not want to make a fool of herself by feeling awkward either. So she successfully avoided seeing him when he called up next time.

'No Meera, not again! You have suffered enough because of your feelings,' she reprimanded herself every time her thoughts drifted to Shimit. Thus, she tried leaving her feelings out in the cold and did not tend to them. But it wasn't a crush that could go away - she did not even feel a need to see or talk to him. In fact, she was quite fine without seeing him. She might not have been strong enough to cut her feelings off but she was restrained enough to curb them.

After four days, she finally gathered some mental strength to call him. His cell phone was switched off. So she called on the landline. The phone rang for a while before the maid picked it up and asked her to wait. Finally, she heard Nandita's voice on the line.

'Hello Aunty, how are you? I just wanted to talk to Shimit.'

'I'm fine *beta*,' she said mechanically. 'Shimit had to go...'

'Where?'

Was there a long pause or did she just imagine it?

'Rajasthan camp near Jaisalmer. There were some reports of unrest on the border. The Army summoned him.'

A long silence followed, terminated by Meera's 'Okay' and gentle click at the hang up button on her phone. In the hours that ensued, her spirit died – one hope at a time.

****

Meera's sensibility took over the reins in due course and she took her parents to visit Nandita to do what little they could to make her feel better. She had hoped for some word that Shimit might have left for her but there was none.

Chapter TWENTY-THREE
Six: Conversation of Light

Three days later, Meera found an email in her inbox that informed her that Dr. Naren was visiting Delhi and she could book an appointment to see him. Was it a signal? She had been longing to talk openly with someone and Dr. Naren seemed just the kind of person she needed. Besides, she was tired of her forlorn self and wanted to seek help from that one person she thought was highly equipped to help her.

She arrived fifteen minutes earlier than the appointed time and was made to wait in the lobby of Radisson where Dr. Naren was staying. At exact 3 pm, she was called in his impeccably clean and modern suite. If it wasn't for his discerning and sage-like countenance that stood quite at contrast to the expensive taste of his ambience, his tailored but simple appearance would not betray Dr. Naren's spiritual inclination. He was dressed like a normal academic personnel but looked the same as he did in Vrindavan - radiant, intellectual and happy. His assistant went to the adjacent room, leaving them comfortably settled in the living room.

After exchanging niceties, he jumped right to the point. 'So, Meera, how are things with you? If I'm seeing you here, I believe you are still seeking him.'

For a moment, she was confused by the mention of 'him' having Shimit in her thoughts but she soon realised that he was picking up their conversation from Iskcon. 'Yes Professor, I'm always seeking him,' she started, not sure how much to reveal.

'By the way, you look liked a changed person.'

Meera smiled thinking of the events that had transpired since their previous visit.

'But that smile has not yet reached its full potential. It is restrained. Why?'

'Why is the smile restrained?' asked Meera.

He nodded donning a faint but encouraging smile himself.

'That's how I smile, I guess.'

'Nonsense. Happy people smile without being conscious and it is like a force of the nature itself - it comes on its own and cannot be controlled by us.'

Meera noticed that he was an animated speaker full of an inner force. If he said something, one would listen to it.

'You are right. I think it's ever since I faced those difficult circumstances in my life. I have become conscious of everything. I know I have moved on but it takes time to forget it, I suppose.'

'Why do you like to carry that burden? On your shoulders, on your lips...'

'I don't want to...and I mostly don't.'

'Let's take that out of your system. Tell me a little about yourself. What are these events that changed your life?'

Meera narrated her story - her love marriage, eventual divorce and social difficulties.

'Tell me everything that you have felt about your circumstances - one sentence at a time and I will interpret it for you.' His face took on the look of a person on a mission.

Meera looked at him, thinking about her life. She felt a mixed sensation of gratitude and nervousness upon such a generous but strange offer.

'No, don't think that much. Close your eyes, transport yourself back to the time when your pains really started or rather you started realising them. Then say whatever comes into your head. Don't overthink and manufacture it, just let it flow.'

She nodded in understanding. Knitting her eyebrows together, she replayed her life backwards to the point her marriage had started falling apart as her eyes looked far away.

'Everything that I could have possibly wanted in life is here. I have a beautiful home, a husband who was my college sweetheart, great job and great financial security. But love is missing, my marriage is incomplete.'

Dr. Naren said in a dispassionate voice - 'I have a convenient life but no happiness. I acknowledge that happiness is higher than convenience. Go on.'

Meera thought about what he had said, hesitated and continued, 'I feel lonelier when my husband is around. He is not even looking at me.'

'I am reading the signals which tell me there is something wrong with my married life. Go on.'

'What's wrong with me?'

'Now that I'm courageous enough to not ignore my relationship failure, I should be strong enough to try to reason and rectify it.'

'But I tried, it still did not work!' Meera's voice had unconsciously risen in pain.

'There's only so much one can rectify. Remember, the law of efforts. When you have failed once, it requires a disproportionately higher percentage of effort to go back where you wanted to be. For example, let's say you started at level 100 and wanted to reach to level 150. You needed 50% more efforts. Now, let's say, your failure brought you down to level 50. Now, to reach to level 150, you don't just need 100% more, 50 original and 50 that you just lost, you actually need 200% more. So what you could not achieve earlier became much harder to reach once you have failed. It is not impossible - no, and people have done it - but that needs determination. In a marriage, it takes two to be compatible. Both of you needed that 200% effort after your failure. Next time you failed, you might now need 400% more. It is just going to increase every time you failed. That's why it is harder to make a failed relationship work because it's not just more effort, it's more effort required not by one person but two. And if they had that much sense, they would probably never have gotten to this point. Accepting failure needs courage too.' His face bore a serious expression.

Meera had closed her eyes during the lengthy reply and was trembling as every word of it reminded her how painful those efforts had become towards the end.

Despite her state, Dr. Naren persisted, 'Go on.'

She tried to focus once again. 'I feel that people judge me about not putting in enough efforts.'

His voice had approached a mocking tone now, 'I want to please everyone. But I should know that's not how life works. If I feel I did not put enough efforts, I can always go back. Do I want to?'

The answer came in without any hesitation, 'No!'

'Then, don't worry what people think. Stop caring and trying to please everyone. You have been given a shape by God and you can't peg yourself into the hole created by others if you are different. Don't distort yourself, be content in standing out. Passing judgments is a tool for people to weaken others on a moral ground. Judgments allow people to banish others who have dared to do something they wanted but couldn't or something that they know is courageous but they don't have the largesse to admire. Who has given anyone the authority to judge? God doesn't judge, your well wishers will never judge, your teachers will never judge. There is nothing good or bad about a decision as long as you accept its responsibility with dignity. You saw a reason and you took action. Why do you seek to explain and bother on being judged? The fact is that to judge is the sign of a weak spirit but to be affected by others' judgments is the sign of a weaker spirit. I don't think you are weak. Are you?'

'No.'

'And you said you *feel* people are judging you. Have they said anything or do you just infer that?'

She was confounded and a bit taken aback. 'Does it matter? I guess they are not going to say it to me, but I can feel it.'

'Then you are judging yourself. We infer mostly what we want things to mean. It's one of our deadliest mistakes. A person in love always hears his love interest to mean that she is reciprocating his love. You expect people to judge and that's why you feel they are judging. And even if you are right, face it and talk to them instead of escaping and complaining behind their back.'

The ruthless words stung her but she knew he was right.

His softer tone resumed on seeing her neck bowing in shame, 'You cannot have one foot in the shore of your past and one on the boat to your future. You have to let one of them go. Which one it will be is your call, but a call needs to be taken.'

'Yes. It's just that it hurts at times.'

'Of course it will and what's wrong with it? Pain is nature's way of telling you to act to heal something. Blessed are those who are given this chance by him.'

Meera looked at him inquisitively, 'What do you mean? Blessed are those who get to feel pain?'

'Yes, imagine what would happen if there was no pain. Would you try to change anything? If your life was uninspired but not really painful, would you have come back?'

The magic potion of his words began untying the knots in her stomach. She sat still.

He continued, 'Are you not happier today? You were thinking of ending your life a year ago. Imagine if you had. You are already living a bonus life, what is there to be afraid of now? This is a chance very few people get. Live your life the way you always wanted. Most of the people spend their whole lives not knowing what real happiness is or what it could be. They are not pushed over the edge, so they keep living without improving anything. But you have been blessed with this realisation. Now are you going to cry to go back to that what you wanted to end or will you accept this blessing and make the most of it?'

Meera was wordless. She had not heard anyone compliment her on her seemingly pathetic situation before and it felt good. And it was true. We tend to be unhappy wherever we are and wanting to go somewhere else. One cannot be happy until one learns to be happy with one's present. She did not see a highly learned scholar in front of her, she was seeing a spiritual mentor who was guiding her towards a future that looked promising just because he seemed to indicate so. Was this destiny? Was she hallucinating? It did not matter because her heart had already given the answer.

'Yes, I will live this second chance and make it the life I wanted.'

His face relaxed as if he was himself released from a great pain. And then, Meera remembered what he had said in Vrindavan - "A spiritual leader will suffer for his pupil's sins." Two tears gently rolled down her cheek as she realised what it feels like to be blessed with a true Guru. Without going into theatricals, she had silently accepted him as her Guru from that moment. She knew she had and would keep passing on her pains to him, she only hoped that there would be fewer in the future.

For the first time he smiled, perhaps in acknowledgment to her thoughts. 'Hope is good. Expectation is not. If you just hoped it would be a good life when you loved, you would be okay if it didn't happen. But if you expected it would be a perfect life when you married and it wasn't, you would be disappointed. Failure does not matter on its own unless you despair because of it. Unhappiness springs from disappointment which itself springs from expectation. Expectation carries the burden of results while hope is weightless. Learn to live, love and laugh. Enjoy where you stand in life without comparing to others.'

****

Meera said with sudden animation, 'What about Krsna?'

'What about him?'

'Why did I see him?'

'Tell me what exactly you see.'

Meera narrated some of her visions and conversations but held on to the dream she saw on her way back from Vrindavan.

'Have you been reading a lot?'

'I guess so.'

'The scenes you describe are inspired from something you have read or heard or watched. Seeing Radha grow in size when Krsna left for Mathura is an inspiration from Yugandhar. The Kaliya dance is described at various places. When you see him on battlegrounds, it is coming from your desire to hear the Gita from him. When you see him meditating as you did often, perhaps it came from your own unfulfilled desire to be able to reach your higher consciousness. He is telling you the words your subconscious wants to tell you. Does that sound plausible?'

Meera remained silent and immobile.

He continued, 'In your solitude, your mind and heart constructed a refuge for you - to tell yourself what you thought you wanted to be told and made Krsna your medium because you have faith in him.'

She was once again, out of words. And again, in tears. 'So, it's not Krsna who I see?'

He put his hand gently on her shoulder. 'Didn't I tell you not to fool yourself into believing that we 'do' things? Nothing happens without the divine will. He wanted you to see him and that's why you saw him. Was he himself there or did he find a way for you to see him nonetheless - how does it matter? As I said, you are the chosen one.'

She closed her eyes and shook her head as if it was all too much to take at once.

Dr. Naren was now smiling playfully, 'Even your physical description is what you wanted him to look as a hero. You know why you don't see his facial details?'

She had no more capacity to reason, she again shook her head - slowly this time.

'Because no definition could match your expectations of what he 'should' look like. He is your spiritual hero and you wanted your hero to be attractive - muscular, tall, charismatic. In a way I'm relieved to know you didn't see blue eyes or blonde hair to make him a Hollywood hero.'

She was truly flabbergasted at the way he laughed. But she blushed admitting the truth in his statements. Yes, she had, in a way, found companionship in Krsna when her life had become wholly doomed and her preferences had influenced what she saw. Once the truth became so simple, she found his joke funny and laughed out herself. She said, 'I don't know about blonde hair but there was a possibility I might have seen him wearing a black cape. I like Christian Bale in *The Dark Knight*.'

'Yes, that was a good movie.'

'What? You watch movies? I mean, I really didn't think someone like you would enjoy those.'

'I'm not a *sannyasi* you know and I don't intend to be. I enjoy living and deriving pleasure from it without indulging in the bonds. It's funny that people often associate spirituality with renunciation. When Arjun, the perfect human, did not become a *sannyasi* on hearing the Gita first hand from Lord Himself, how can one infer that Lord asks us to abandon everything? The Gita reconciles practical life and our goal of liberation beautifully. It tells you how, by indulging in devotion in practical terms and dedicating all our *karmas* to God, we can get rid of the cycle of rebirths. Just as a boat floats on water, gets wet on the outside but does not let the water come inside, so shall we live in this world being touched by it externally but not let it change our inner self. I don't tie myself to a particular school of thought as I have developed my own consciousness over the years but the Gita comes close to being the consummate philosophy.'

"Yajnaarthaat karmano'nyatra loko'yam karmabandhanah;

Tadartham karma kaunteya muktasangah samaachara.[38]*"*

Meera's thoughts inevitably went back to Bhanudas and whatever she had witnessed about karma. Her face tightened up in an unknown tension.

'Have you read the Gita?' he enquired.

'Yes I have tried upon my father's recommendation.'

'Good. You should listen to him. Actually he can tell you everything that I can but his foible is that he is a father. It's natural for him to be emotionally biased and in any case, you will always underplay what he says because he is your father,' he said with the same mystic smile she had often seen on her father's face.

She started as it felt like he was reading all her thoughts. He was so right - we tend to take our family for granted without giving them the due importance and credit. She added, 'I have vowed to listen to him. It's just that I feel I make him weak and I don't like it.'

---

[38] If anyone does actions for the sake of the Lord, he is not bound. O son of Kunti, perform action for that sake of sacrifice alone, free from attachment!

'Of course you make him weak, but don't forget you are also his strength – a much larger strength than a weakness. It's the tragedy of being a girl's father that he is always aware of one fact - that he cannot take care of you forever, howsoever he wants, because it is unnatural. He dreads the day you will go away and yet he wishes that you don't have to stay. You will understand it someday.'

Meera held back her tears. The topic of her parents always made her vulnerable but she found peace in what Dr. Naren had said. In her father, she had seen the epitome of struggle an Indian parent puts up to ensure that his child gets it all - the values, happiness, fulfillment in every possible form. They shared their own mute language. His unsaid torment, inaudible sighs and unrevealed tears were always acknowledged by her with a brave smile - even if she had to force it because she couldn't afford to add to his already mighty burden.

****

Her eyes lowered as she thought about Shimit again.

'I have lost a friend.'

He looked at her as if he knew more was coming.

She shifted once again uncomfortably under his omniscient gaze. 'I had wondered if I'd be able to care for anyone again. I thought I had lost the capacity to have feelings for anyone.'

'Nonsense. No amount of heartbreak should make one resistant to love. But let it be selfless unconditional love - uncaring of the outcome, uncaring of other's response. That's all I would say. You will have to understand and learn it on your own. And I'm confident that you will.'

She understood that he was willing to say no more on the topic. So she let his words stick in her memory for later musing.

He continued, 'Every person you meet has been assigned to play a role in your story as you are assigned to play one in someone else's. I often say that the people we come across can be one of the four kinds. They can be like pebbles, fountains, quagmire or a bridge. Pebbles are those who you meet commonly and in abundance. They do not facilitate anything great but they help you continue walking on this journey of life. Everyone you cross in life without really connecting with are pebbles. Then there are fountains - which spring water of happiness on you. They bring positivity and joy; they nourish your soul and irrigate the seeds of good thoughts. Your friends, well-wishers are all fountains. Then on the other end of the spectrum, you have quagmires. These are the people who cause you pain. Now, even some pebbles may have caused you pain as it happens if you tread on a barbed pebble but the difference is that quagmires do that on purpose. They pull you down, induce fear and negativity by discouraging you and worrying you. They will not let you move on - that's why they keep you bogged down in your failures. Finally, the rarest ones are the bridges - they connect you to unchartered ground that you wouldn't have reached on your own. They unite you to your destiny. With them, your plane of consciousness expands, you see things you have not seen before; your life becomes more aware, more enlightened. Your parents, your teachers and anyone who touches your life and transcends it into something more beautiful - they are all bridges.'

An impressed Meera smiled in appreciation.

He carried on, 'And you also perform the same functions in someone else's life. To certain extent, we also determine who will be whom in our life. You can promote some of your fountains to bridges by giving back to them some value. Our good deeds bring more bridges and there I have connected the Gita with my philosophy.' He grinned.

'That was so beautifully put.'

'Similarly, every episode of your life has a purpose. Your being in India has been orchestrated by something or someone. Else, how do you explain it? You answered to a calling when you made that decision, but don't be ignorant enough to think that it was a work of your mind alone. You were directed back to India because this is where you belonged right now. You can either choose to ignore that higher purpose or you can embrace it - your spirit, destiny, karma, God, calling - whatever it is. It is present everywhere for everyone. It is directing everyone but not everyone is tuned in to hear it. Just like a radio. When you tune it to the right frequency, you can hear whatever the station is playing clearly. Even though it's still playing it all the time, you won't hear it unless you are on the right frequency. Same applies to our spiritual tuning. Think, there is a spiritual station playing at some xyz frequency. When you elevate your consciousness and thereby tune in to that frequency, you start hearing the messages. You tuned in, now don't tune out. Follow the calling of your heart.'

'I have already made you my Guru and I'm sorry I'll be causing you pain. But please accept me as your disciple.'

'I accepted you the day we met. We meet today not by chance. Live and find peace.'

****

After a lot of back and forth in her mind, Meera had finally found the conviction to discuss one thing she had not mentioned so far to anyone - her bizarre dream. She felt that he was the only person she could share it with.

'What is it?' he asked reading her knitted brows.

She briefly narrated her encounter and it was only by the thoughtful probing of her teacher that she excavated the finer details from remote corners of her memory that she was frankly, nervous to touch on her own.

The narration had impressed him beyond imagination and he sat silent for couple of minutes. Meera did not move either.

'I wonder why you call it a dream. This is simply extraordinary. And you remember all those fine details.'

'But it is disturbing.'

'Why?'

'It might sound crazy but the way it ended bothers me. I was left stranded. I didn't get to meet Krsna. All this while when I used to see him, I felt I had a connection but apparently He didn't want me to see him? Has he abandoned me? I have not seen him ever since...' her eyes betrayed a deep sense of hurt over desertion. 'Frankly, I had not even thought of it till now but now that I'm talking to you, I realise how much it bothers me.'

'Then, you yourself know that it wasn't a dream. One thing is clear, you need to face that experience and find a way to bring it to a close. You don't need help with it and I don't even think I or anyone else can really help you. You know that already.'

They looked at each other.

He continued, 'If he has led you this far, he will show you the way too. But you need to show up for it. I can understand it was an awe-inspiring experience but precious one, nonetheless. Embrace it. Face it as you have faced everything in life - with dignity and resolute. What are you afraid of?'

'Failure that I may not find him and that I have lost him too.'

'Ah. Who else have you lost, my dear?'

Her eyes flickered. He did not wait for her answer.

'Love is not about possessing someone. Love is a special form of faith and no one else but you control it. Don't worry about losing anyone, it is that fear that prevents you from loving whole heartedly. And half hearted devotion won't do. If you love him, go all in and he will have no option but to reveal himself. Love is that powerful.'

They spoke very little afterwards and when Meera felt the assurance she was looking for, she got up to leave. She tried to touch his feet but he stopped her. He put his hand on her head. 'And, don't let anyone turn you away from your visions. What do they know? You have seen Krsna and whichever form he is in, no one can change the fact that he lets you see him. Even I can't explain it. Maybe I'm ignorant and you are here to teach me how to believe. So, never give up on faith. God bless you, Meera.'

As Meera stepped out of the door, she looked back and said, 'I hope I am a fountain for you.'

He replied, 'No, you are a bridge.'

****

Meera felt light - the lightness that one feels when one has shared a deeply kept secret with someone. She knew in her subconscious that her dream revelation was so powerful that she had found herself unprepared for it. But today Dr. Naren's company and words had given her a light that could guide her on her quest to finish her so-called internship successfully. She needed to pass the test, for the result was a high stake one. She knew if she succeeded, she would find him too. And she did want to find him.

Her parents were waiting for her when she entered the home with a smile. She went straight and hugged her Dad tight. He was taken aback for they were not a very expressive family but this was probably the kind of signal he had been waiting for. He hugged her back warmly without saying a single word. Then, she went to hug and kiss her mother who embraced her as she always did.

'I love you, Ma.'

'I love you, *meri bachchi*,' she said with a kiss on her forehead.

As they sat down for dinner, Meera noticed that *okra* was in the menu. And, she had not been served *okra* because she had developed distaste for it in her childhood. It is one of those things that you just tend to remember from childhood. She didn't even care why she didn't like it anymore except that she wouldn't eat it, no matter what. And thereafter, whenever Amrita cooked *okra*, she had to cook another vegetable just for Meera. Amrita had tried unsuccessfully to make her eat it many a times and had eventually given up.

But tonight somehow her tastes or preferences did not matter. Her thoughts went to that middle aged paralysed man who she had seen with Bhanudas and who performed his duties and led a simple life. He did not care for the pains or preferences - he just surrendered all his actions unto him. How can you win over your pain until you can learn to win over your desires?

She picked up the spoon and served herself some *okra*. And, she ate it without a grimace or frown. It was a new taste for her and she had already made up her mind to like it.

Amrita was shocked and if it wasn't for the peaceful expression on Meera's face, she would have been very worried. Instead, she found herself immersing in the happiness that Meera was exuding. Sumer recognised a transformation when he saw one. At this moment, seeing the piety and enlightenment on her daughter's face transcended any pleasure any pilgrimage had ever given him. Any doubts that he had about Meera's decision to end her marriage and leave a flourishing career in New York were laid to rest today. Forever.

Chapter TWENTY-FOUR

Unconquerable Soul

When she got up the next morning, it was drizzling. Meera sipped her ginger tea leisurely on the balcony, watching the raindrops dance on the leaves and slide down merrily. Most of the days in our life are dull; sadly unremarkable. And some, plain bad. Amidst these lackluster days, once in a while, comes a spirited day such as the one in front of her today. The spring in the air seeped into her being and washed off the dust of her loneliness.

In twenty minutes, she was out carrying her umbrella and camera and sauntering in a nearby park. Although it had stopped raining, the mist suspended in the air made her feel like she was walking through a cloud. She loved the rains and the squeaky clean green leaves that smiled afterwards. Switching her camera on, she took some macro shots of roses, lilies, butterflies and grass - yes, grass with dew drops beats the beauty of the most admired flowers just like walking on wet grass with naked feet beats the heavenliness of the most poetic feeling.

She settled on a bench to review the photos she had just taken and her fingers froze as soon as the back button displayed the picture of Shimit. All the feelings about him that she had put aside came rushing back. She was angry that her uncalled-for feelings had tainted the very sacred relation of friendship she held with him. And how could she ever forgive herself for not seeing him one last time before he left?

One thing was clear - her effort at denying her feelings for him was not going to work.

So why was she trying to deny it anyway? Wasn't it beautiful that she hadn't lost the capacity to have feelings after a failed marriage? That she could love again meant she was still very much alive - wasn't that something to celebrate rather than be embarrassed about?

And then the thoughts of that afternoon in the barn came rushing back to her. The conversation afterwards and her realisation of deeper feelings had completely eclipsed the phenomenal revelation she had witnessed in the barn. Shimit had taught her how to make her heart talk and now she was trying to suppress that same heart.

At that moment her eyes fell on a peacock that had just emerged in a far corner of the garden. Within a blink of her eye, he had fanned open his brilliant plumage and begun dancing. The feathers swayed in the wind as he twirled around in circles. She stood captivated by the flaunt of his splendor for the next couple of minutes. When he finally folded his plumage and vanished behind the bushes, Meera walked to the spot. As if she knew what she was going to find, she looked intently at the lone stem of peacock feather that lay there, inviting her to examine its outrageously bright colors. She picked it up and caressed the strands delicately, staring at its iridescent eye. 'You do not belong here, you are meant to adorn the One who has sent you here,' mumbled Meera.

The wind slowly began to pick up speed and it was as if she was being sent a message that her eyes closed in obedience.

A vision of Radha unfolded before her eyes; she was standing on the banks of the Yamuna alone. She held a *morpankh* and a flute casually in her hands and the same resplendent smile occupied her lips that Meera had always seen on her. She neither looked lonely nor wanting. And when Meera had further focused, hundreds of reflections of Krsna had emerged within Radha's form.

Meera knew what Dad had meant by calling Radha the *shakti* of Krsna. She also knew why she looked so happy and peaceful. She no longer had any questions about the undefined relationship of Radha-Krsna, she had understood that no mortal possessed the capability to define it. Radha personified love in its purest form - the unconditional love that doesn't depend on being formalized into a relationship or fulfilled. Pure love is always strong enough to flourish on its own.

And wasn't Shimit's love for that girl the same too? Unadulterated and absolute. That is what Dr. Naren had meant as well. Suddenly, she was no longer embarrassed about her feelings for Shimit or conscious of the fact that they would always remain unreciprocated. Neither was she sad. She was understanding pure love and feeling privileged to know how it felt.

The clouds had begun roaring and she felt nature's embrace in the gust of wind that followed. Yes, she was a part of it. Wherever there are dark clouds, there's bright lightening. Wherever there's thunder, there's the melody of raindrops. Wherever there's pain, there's hope.

It began pouring before she had a chance to open her umbrella. She wouldn't have, anyway. She stood there to get drenched, to be cleansed of every negative feeling and pain until only love remained - love for life and everything in it - untouched of longing, expectations or possession.

And, then she saw Krsna.

He was totally engrossed in playing the flute under a tree as rain fell heavily all around him. Her heart leapt with joy - it felt like a lost fawn had found her mother back in the herd. She stared, her gaze steadfast, 'I'm not letting you go. I will keep calling you when I'm in pain. I will call you when I'm overjoyed. I will call you when I feel full of love. I will call you in every breath of mine. I will find you no matter what.' She turned her head up to the sky and let the raindrops kiss her.

****

She ran up to her room lest her wet clothes and body drench the whole house. She changed, wrapped her wet hair in a towel and set upon her task on the laptop. After an hour, she was standing at a digital studio and collecting the prints she had ordered. After another hour, she was chatting with the owner of Cafe Pallette. He was only slightly older than her but his arrogance added another five years to his appearance. He had listened to her request quietly.

'I'm sorry we don't allow newbies,' came the flat rejection.

Meera sat silent for few moments before opening her second line of attack. 'Are you a self-made man, Mr. Shiraz?'

His eyes did not conceal the surprise at the unexpected question. But he took time to grasp it. 'Yes, I did not inherit this place if that's what you mean.'

'Then you very well know what it is to hustle and how grateful we feel when someone helps us. You must also have had your first time at everything you are an expert at now.'

He sighed and Meera knew that meant that she had broken the armour of indifference.

'I get that but I'm not going to melt with your words and open my gallery to you. You have to earn it. Show me one picture that will tell me you are crazy.'

She pursed her lips in contemplation, she knew exactly what he meant, but had to prove herself. She flipped through the pictures she was carrying in her bag, picked the one she wanted to show him and slid it across the table.

He glanced at it casually, then squinted to look at the tiny details. She explained to him what it was. He listened patiently.

Once she was done, he slid the picture back to her and got up.

'If you need time to think it over, I can wait outside,' said Meera desperately hoping to get a positive response.

'I don't need time. I recognise madness when I see it. I will let you do this exhibition - it's a chance I almost never give easily, so I hope you'll make it count.'

She nodded without smiling. Just as she had reached the door, she turned back remembering something very important.

'Where did you get the WereWoman from?'

'The painting?'

She nodded impatiently.

'Why?'

She thought for a second. 'I want it...'

He smiled. 'I bought it from Spain, it's my favorite.'

She sighed; she knew what that word meant to her prospects of asking him to give it to her.

'Umm...I really really want it. Not because I'm an art connoisseur or collector but because I am one of those women in the picture.' She paused, thinking of the best way to express it, eventually giving in to just raw emotions that were surging through her, 'As crazy as it may sound, I... I need it. I...'

'Which one of those women are you?' he asked looking intently at her expressive and struggling eyes.

She smiled because that question meant he understood what she was talking about. 'Right now, I think I'm in between the two. I have unfettered myself but am yet to reach the boat.'

He thought and said, 'It's expensive.'

'Oh...I'll try to manage.' She had not even thought how, but she knew that she was desperate enough to think something up.

He started trotting around the room, his restless gait and thoughtful bent of head revealing his dilemma. Finally he paused and looked up with lips pursed in sympathy. Meera knew what he was going to say, so she ventured herself, 'It's okay. I understand it's not a painting one would want to part with.'

He was taken aback at her graceful acceptance. 'Wait a minute,' he said and moved to his chair. For the next few minutes, he was busy excavating stuff from his drawers. Ultimately, he looked up and offered her a postcard in his hand. It was a miniature replica of the WereWoman with the name and the address of the artist whose painting it was. It read Aaron Perez. Meera accepted it with heartfelt admiration. 'Thank you.'

'Why do you want it so badly?'

'Everyone has her own perception of happiness. Looking at that painting delighted me in an inexplicable way. I wanted to own that delight.'

He understood what she meant. 'So, I'll see you next week.'

'Next week it is.'

****

The next day, Meera paid a visit to Nandita to see how she was doing. They chatted for quite some time. Over the last few visits, Meera had started understanding Nandita's likes, dislikes, what she feared and what made her happy. In the process, she had begun admiring her more for the courage with which she fought the adversities. Some people have powerful presence and Nandita was one of them. Her steady eyes, well-kept appearance and propriety could be daunting to outsiders but Meera had now understood how to look beyond it to the soft core of a mother's heart. They had started opening out to each other and Nandita found solace in her presence.

During one lazy afternoon, Nandita shared the latest updates about Shimit. She had read his letter dispassionately but Meera knew the courage it took her to not burst into tears. The delicate situation still prevailed on the border and Shimit was likely to be held up until the tension calmed down.

Then unexpectedly she began looking at some abstract spot on the wall, 'Shimit is a good boy.'

Meera was taken aback momentarily and found herself out of words upon looking at the faraway expression in Nandita's eyes.

But soon she came back to the present and requested Meera to look for a book in Shimit's room that she wanted to read.

It was after a long time that Meera had seen Shimit's room - it lacked any decorations and was full of medical books. As she went through his table drawers, her fingers paused on a personal diary. She knew she shouldn't be looking inside but she picked it up and flipped it open nonetheless. It was from two years ago. To her utter disappointment, it was empty.

Just as she was going to close and put it back, she thought she saw some writing on a page. Then she noticed that few random pages had been written on. It was scribbled with Urdu *shayari* and its translation. She knew Shimit was a big fan of poetry, so she thought that the diary was a collection of his favorite couplets. She opened the page of July 18, 2010 and read it.

Muqaam 'Faiz' koi raah mein jacha hi nahin
Jo koo-e-yaar se nikle to soo-e-daar chale

None of the rest areas appealed to me on the way. As I left from the lane of my beloved, I headed straight to the gallows.

She felt a pang of grief as the thought of him standing in the Army camp shook her.

'He must have written this when he had decided to take up the fellowship offer and...chose not to propose...,' she thought looking at the date.

She flipped open next written page on Sep 03, 2010 that read -

Chaand nikle kisi jaanibh, teri zebaai ka
Rang badle kisi soorat shab-e-tanhayi ka

The moon of your beauty, I hope, will emerge in some direction. The beauty that cannot be captured by any worthy metaphor, the moon being the only closest option. Such is the beauty of my love. I long to see that beauty sometime so that the color and appearance of this night of solitude may change. The night of solitude that can't be anything but painful and dark can only brighten up by the emergence of a moon of your grace.

The words floated in her eyes bringing an onslaught of despair and empathy. He didn't get the one he loved. And she would never get the one she does.

The entry on Sep 19, 2010 read-

Kar raha tha gham-e-jahaan ka hisaab
Aaj tum yaad be-hisaab aaye
Is tarah apni khaamoshi goonji
Goya har simt se jawaab aaye

It had no translation. Meera could feel the utter distress in those words and anxiously flipped ahead. Dec 17, 2010 read -

Jo ruke toh koh-e-garan the hum, jo chale to jaan se guzar gaye
Rah-e-yaar hum ne qadam qadam, tujhe yadgaar bana dia

When we stopped, we were as firm and unyielding as a difficult mountain; when we walked, we became larger than life, we gave the momentum to the cause. And with every step we progressed, we made this whole journey a testament of our struggle and sacrifices. It is not the hard journey that gave us recognition but the other way round.

Meera re-read it multiple times with tears welling up in her eyes. This last couplet probably summed up Shimit in his entirety. The rest of the diary was empty.

The sparse diary was the witness of his struggle and journey as he had risen from personal feelings to a bigger cause. It was not possible to respect him more but she did. She kept the diary back in its place and started looking back for Nandita's book.

****

Meera was standing at the entrance to receive the first guests on the last day of her exhibition at Cafe Pallette. She was exhibiting the photographs from her numerous travels from New York and

India. The next visitor entered with a broad smile and a beautiful pink carnation in his hand. He was wearing a *kurta* but had no *teeka* on his forehead this time.

She hugged Madhur, accepting the pretty flower delicately, 'Thanks for coming.'

'My pleasure. Your invitation came as a pleasant surprise and I wouldn't have turned it down. Besides, I was intrigued to see how photographers look.'

'Because you didn't really know how I looked?'

'No, I didn't know how you looked *as a photographer.*'

'So how do the photographers look? - what's your verdict?'

'Don't know about *photographers* but the one I'm seeing looks resplendent. And if it's the magic of doing this exhibition, then I shall start practicing photography myself.'

She chuckled. 'Stop pulling my leg.'

'I hear you are creating ripples in the artistic lanes of Delhi. That was a sweet review in the HT city edition.'

'Oh now, don't exaggerate. That article appeared because a close friend of mine has good media contacts. But yes, the exhibition has been better than what I was dreading. I thought I'd be swatting flies here, but the turnout has been good so far.'

'Aren't you going to show me your photos?'

They went in and she gave him a special tour with commentary that she had perfected by now. But she did not have to say anything when they stood in front of a photo on the extreme right - it was a meticulously taken macro shot of a peacock feather. They smiled in mutual understanding before moving on.

'You love lighthouses, don't you? I have seen at least ten different ones in here.'

She nodded. 'Yeah, they fascinate me. Whenever I see one, I think of the dark thunderous nights when its flickering light guided the ancient ships sailing in utter darkness. Its lamp must have brought hope to lost ships and its dysfunction might have caused a shipwreck. Everyone needs a guiding light, don't they?'

Madhur lingered around a photo with considerable interest as Meera attended a couple of inquisitive guests. A sleeping koala displaying a picayune bent of head, nestled in between the prongs of the eucalyptus tree.

'I'm happy to discover that you have finally found something captivating enough,' said Meera returning to him.

'You know what this makes me think of?'

'What?'

'It reminds me of monks meditating in zen. Unruffled and serene.'

'Ah. Then, I shall name it 'Bear of Zen'!'

'Getting the viewer to pay more attention to your piece can only be artfully deserved and not begged for. You have a knack for storytelling, these photographs are absolutely thought provoking and not something I would just *glance through and get it over with*.'

She was touched by the spontaneity of his compliment and smiled self-effacingly.

'So which one can I afford?'

'Nah, you don't have to be that sweet. I just appreciate that you came.'

'No really, I would like to buy this koala one.'

'Hmm...why don't you buy me a good coffee and I give you that photo?'

'You serious?'

'Absolutely.'

'That sounds an amazing deal. Done.'

'Cool.'

'And if you keep doing business like that, you will soon be broke,' he broke into a handsome grin.

****

As Meera was wrapping up her equipment and frames at the end of the day, Shiraz walked in.

'Congratulations...that was one of the most successful exhibitions we have had. You got great feedback.'

'Yes, I can hardly believe it,' she said without holding back any excitement.

'Listen, I came to tell you that you can buy that painting from me. I would have given it just like that but it's kind of expensive.'

Her hands paused the incessant packing and she looked up at him in disbelief. Her expression softened immediately, 'You know what, I know what it's like to own something you love. I don't want you to give it up. I have found my muse in my photographs... But thanks so much for your offer. Just allow me to walk in anytime to look at that painting.'

A brief silence ensued as the two art lovers appreciated each other's viewpoint.

'I can allow that on one condition.'

'What's that?'

'Your next exhibition will be held here only.'

She grinned, 'I can do that.'

'And I think you have successfully transformed to the girl in the golden rays,' he said and left without waiting for her to respond.

The empty gallery stood in darkness except for the focused light on the last remaining photo encased in the biggest frame in the center on the flawless white wall. It was the picture of 'Bell and Faces'. Meera stepped a foot away from it beholding it in her proud gaze. She had packed all the photos but this one; it demanded special attention. Recognising fully that the only reason she was standing here today savoring her newfound success was one man: the only man she wished was standing here with her and the only man who couldn't make it.

****

Later that night, she strolled out into the garden and kept walking till a late hour.

Shimit's words came back to her – "Make yourself feel accomplished again." He was so right. Amidst all the uncertainties in her life, she felt truly happy by that tiny success of her exhibition. That was the feeling of accomplishment he was talking about. She knew he would have been happiest to see her today. That made her smile, part in love and part in tragedy. Despite all the longing, she didn't forget to thank God in her thoughts. Somehow, she was feeling Krsna's presence particularly stronger tonight. When it came to Shimit, she felt helpless but she felt more optimistic about Krsna now - at least she could try finding him.

But how? She did not know. And when she did not know what else to do, she often turned to traveling. She was a wanderer at heart. Sometimes, the best way to find yourself is to wander and get lost.

Chapter TWENTY-FIVE

Seven: Conversation of Self

Early the next morning, she prepared to leave for the destination she only knew by name and by the approval of her heart.

'Sorry Ma, forgot to tell you about the impromptu plan, but am really looking forward to this trek.'

'Yes, I'll be back soon but don't panic if you can't contact me. I am expecting weak cell reception there, I'll call whenever I can.'

'No, you can't come Ma.'

She kissed her mother's cheek just before leaving and wanted to tell how important this was to her but she didn't want to freak her out. She conveniently omitted that it was a solitary trek. And that she had planned it to be spent literally in silence. And that she had self-imposed a rule of photography abstinence. Traveling often rescued her but this one was slightly different than her earlier attempts. She wasn't trying to escape her problems or distract herself with photography. Her purpose was to remove everything between her and whatever bigger phenomenon existed out there - be it her voice, discord, material distractions and above all her doubts. This was her excursion into the depths of her own self where she knew what awaited - the divine truth and key to finding him.

She was headed to the mighty Himalayas. Not because mystics had discovered some sacred truths in those altitudes or that one could expect to find *sannyasis* in a forsaken cave; no, she needed a perspective. And what else but the grandiose of lofty Himalayan peaks could offer her that perspective? She hoped she was right and that she would be able to unlock her answers mysteriously when she had reached the right height. She was truly on her own now and she was curious to see how she would react.

As she stepped out into the chatter of birds, she could feel the importance of this dawn in her life. It would bring something new - either the answers she looked for or disappointment. Either way it would help her move forward - that seemed a goal worth striving for. It was a long journey. The delicate red light began to brighten as her journey proceeded through curvy railway tracks followed by dusty country roads. There was something about the changing greenery and receding feel of civilization that made Meera smile as she looked out of the window like a curious child. Far ahead the Himalayas loomed, growing taller by the minute. The tracks turned uphill and the car engines whirred to overcome the gravity.

'No, we are not going to be in the Himalayas but you are going to view its peaks up close. It's a sight you will never forget,' the driver answered her queries with a confident smile.

The road journey climaxed with a pristine village, Sari, nestled in between thick forests from where the trek began. Meera tagged along with a group of hikers without mingling too much on the pretext of a sore throat. The paved pathway offered little challenge to an accustomed climber but provided a good warm up to Meera who had not hiked much in recent years. She curiously touched the rich brown barks of the cedars and pines, occasionally smiling at carved out hearts pierced with arrows of the adolescent lovers. She breathed deeply to let the mountain air reach far within every cell of her body.

Suddenly the forest cleared to a flat land and a sight she would never forget. The still waters of Deoriya Tal amidst a luscious green expanse mirrored the far away snowy peaks so splendidly that she felt like kneeling down and offering her prayers to the nature and its display of grandeur.

'That white beauty is the Chaukhamba - the mountain massif in Himalayan range,' explained a fellow hiker who was returning for his umpteenth visit. She did not know what a massif meant but it sounded magical - just what she was searching for.

The nature had primed the canvas for a perfect sunset as they reached closer to the lake. The westerly sun rolled out layers of shadows until only the defiant Himalayan peaks – the four jagged horns of Chaukhamba, Kedar Range, Nilkantha and many others – emerged bronze in the setting sun. The evening shroud rapidly darkened into prussian blues of night under a staggeringly starry sky. She had a basic meal at the only facility on the camping site and left the excited hikers singing around the campfire to walk about the lake.

The moon waxed to its fullest position atop the mountains. She sat down on a mound of grass and leaned back on her palms to get a comfortable angle for star sighting. She had barely spoken twenty words in the day and her heart felt as silent as the nature at this altitude. The stars winked at her as her head went the full 360 degrees watching the endless expanse of unobstructed sky. Her eyes traced shapes between them, drawing an unimagined joy and wonder. The altitude, her silence and 'stripped out to essentials' mode of existence made her feel incredibly close to the ultimate force whose calling had beckoned her. She slipped back to lie flat and stare at infinity; never before had she witnessed such fiery stars and magnificent constellations. She rolled over a couple of times until every pore on her skin had felt the touch of icy but heavenly grass.

As she sat back up, her eyes captured the most spellbinding sight she had ever encountered in front - the bluish silhouette of Chaukhamba had advanced awfully close at night - only if she could extend her hand to touch it. The snow- straddled peaks appeared lighter against the ever-growing dark sky and she stared and stared to savor every last bit of the rare vista that had unfolded before her.

Many a time her hands reached for her camera but she refrained – it was not a sight to be drunk through the glass of any lens. The last time she had felt anything close to this experience was when she had gazed at the Southern Alps range in New Zealand. But she was a different self back then - her soul was too murky to talk to the mountain and the wind. Today she would. She stood up and walked to the other side of the lake towards the peaks, closer to the edge.

She felt a transmission of awe and force through her as if she was communicating with the elements of life that constituted her body. Standing amidst the earth, water, air, fire and sky in their primal physical form, she could feel she was absorbing a tremendous energy and emitting a fusion of it - that then echoed between the walls of these mountains, resulting in a resonance of euphoria. Her body and this universe were all part of the same cosmic immanence. Instead of feeling tiny and meaningless in front of the gigantic geography, she felt herself raised to magnificent proportions because she was a part of it.

****

After a short but effective sleep in her cozy sleeping bag, she got up early to catch the first rays of the sun. Meera had no clue that nature had elaborate plans to keep astounding her but that is such a petty word. In general one associates 'astounding' with an unexpected fact or unanticipated beauty of an experience but it cannot do justice to the powers that were manifest here. The language is not equipped to handle such miracles. Behind the silhouettes of the peaks, the maroon and vermillion cracks had begun to emerge. The sorcery of the nature hit the first spell as a fiery ray struck the right side of the mountain range in front, temporarily blazing it up in a golden flame. Within a matter of seconds, the golden lava had spread to the top of all the peaks torching them up. The sun rose smiling in the east.

Soon after some refreshments, the trekkers left for Chandrashila and she followed suit. They crossed a small village and a couple of temples on the winding trail. She paid her respect at the small Shiv temple where Mahadev had taken abode among his favorite landscape - the untouched heights. The remnants of snow from the previous season were all set to welcome the pilgrims that would come barging in the next few weeks. By the noon, the long hike brought them to the 13000 feet high summit that provided a closer view of the Himalayas and spectacular valleys beneath. Following a light lunch and siesta, she set out on a solo exploration. She walked to the edges to see incomprehensible depths and looked to the Himalayas for insurmountable heights. In between the two, she was alone with herself and it was soothing to realise she liked her own company.

Her thoughts soon found their way out fluidly - How much time did it take to create such majestic topology? 50 million or 500 million years? And yet, we humans grow so impatient in a matter of months or years. This is the age of instant gratification; we do not know or want to know the possible outcomes of longer efforts. If God thought like that, we would not have the Himalayas, oceans, volcanoes, evolution, diamonds, oil etc.

She found a patch of few Deodar trees where the sunlight filtering through the woods lit up the ground in uneven patterns. After walking through it for some time, she came out from the other side where the mountain curved to provide another angle into views of magnificent scenery around. She found her perch on a massive boulder protruding from the cliff and closed her eyes, focusing all her attention on her eyelids - it was a technique she knew from yoga. The clouds and bubbles in the eye fluid started creating random patterns in the darkness that shrouded her eyes. Gradually she made herself aware of the rim of her eyelids and every sensation around them, releasing control over them until they felt neither light nor heavy, until they took an identity of their own and it needed willful force to even open them up. The unconscious, unintentional and thoughtless blinking that we do million times a day gave in to a conscious stillness.

She found herself in the City of Justice.

****

She was standing at a town square. Her body felt physically exhausted as she looked around, trying to identify the paths. Finally she pushed her tired limbs and started walking down one alley that she felt led to the enlightenment park. She tried to remember the spot where she had crossed the man in the *dhoti* and shawl. *Yes, she was now looking for him.*

And it hardly took five minutes to locate him this time. As they say, if you know what you are looking for, you will probably find it. He was standing facing away from Meera as she arrived but he immediately turned around and said nonchalantly, 'I have been expecting you for a long time.' He was fair, tall and well built with an angular chiseled face that seemed to emanate a force of invisible power. While she could not place her finger on what exact feature caused it, his overall presence was incredibly dominating and attractive. It was only from close that she realised how tall and big he was; she had to look up to face him. She was mesmerised and lost awareness of everything else in his presence. Somehow she managed to reply, 'I have been looking for you.'

'I know.'

'You are Krsna...'

'I am whoever your faith makes me.'

'You made me come here and experience all this. Why?'

'You were looking for answers with pure intentions. You deserved a little help. Your skepticism springs from a deeper faith that wants to know those answers not for the sake of your questions, but to prove that your faith is right.'

'Chitragupta told me to figure out the purpose of my visit so that I could find a way out from here. But now that I have seen you, why would I ever want to go away? Meeting you is bigger than any purpose I can have.'

He smiled, 'Because the river cannot stop flowing.'

Meera wondered if everyone in this place always talked in riddles.

'I think I'm here to know some answers.'

'Let's start then,' he said and started walking. Meera followed him until they came to a big door. She expected to receive some instructions but he opened the door and vanished behind it silently. She hastened to open the door herself and was about to step in when her feet froze. The door opened into endless water. Stepping in meant drowning in her case. She found him at some distance, walking in water! He paused to look back at her and said, 'Come.'

'How? I can't swim.'

'You didn't think that once before, did you? I had to pull you back at the last moment.'

Meera stared dumbfounded as memories of that dark night came flooding to her mind.

'Come now. There's no water here, it's all in your head.' He started walking away.

Meera panicked and then looked at his receding figure. She did not have even a moment to weigh upon her options, the only determined thought being that she could not lose him this time. And once you make your choice, the options don't matter. Closing her eyes shut, she thrust herself in the vast expanse of water. Now that is the beauty of the first step - you take it and you feel liberated and committed. There was no going back. And as her companion had assured, the water did not seem to be drowning or touching her, she could walk through it. Soon, she caught up with him, staying a few steps behind as he walked briskly.

Next she found him climbing up on some invisible stairs and it's hard to follow anyone on a path that cannot be seen. But it occurred to her that she was already walking and breathing in water, so expecting things out-of-the-way was not a bad idea after all. Something incited her to step out of the water as if there existed another invisible staircase for her. And for sure, she could climb up as casually as she had been walking a moment ago.

As she followed him out of the water, she could see them standing on the shore of a flourishing city. Splendid golden structures and pillars shone at close quarters.

'Long back it sheltered me and my clan. Isn't it beautiful?'

'This is Dwarika, isn't it?' asked Meera burning with curiosity.

He nodded. She tried to find any sign of attachment in his eyes but there was none. He was smiling and simply stating a fact.

He advanced into the royal city and traipsed through the pathways until they reached a palace with bright red *dhvaja* fluttering imperiously on top. In his plain attire he would have looked out of the place in the stately castle, but his comfortable and commanding gait was the very stamp of his ownership on the existence of this kingdom. And that thought only amused Meera as she thought that there was possibly *no* place that he did *not* own. She nearly jumped when the sound of multiple bells tolling in a melodious welcome hit her. The palace was welcoming its King.

'This is Rukmini's room,' he said entering into a large and exquisitely decorated room. They walked up to the beautiful balcony that stretched out overlooking the sea. He continued, 'Dwarika cannot exist without Rukmini. She was the soul of this kingdom. I still remember the plea of help she sent me. Do you know how she came to be my queen?'

Meera shook her head.

'Her marriage was being arranged to another king when she wrote to me to abduct her and accept her as my wife. And do you know how well she knew me at that time?'

She again shook her head.

'She had never met me.' He added, 'Can faith get any stronger? Can love be any more submissive? Giving is still easy but you know what is harder?'

She stared, trying to comprehend the meaning of those words.

He had rested one hand against the pillar over his head and let his body lean on it and his bent leg. His other hand rested handsomely on his waist as he assumed the well-known majestic tri-bent stance. 'Asking is hard. And, asking to be loved is hardest, especially for anyone with a speck of ego.'

She could not agree more. 'How can one ask to be loved? Love has to be deserved, isn't it?'

He smiled the most enthralling smile. 'What are those but pretexts to cover one's fear of being rejected in love? If one's love is sincere, why should it depend on being accepted or not. Only the fearless and selfless can declare their love and more so, ask to be accepted.'

'But asking something for oneself even if it is to be loved - how can that be selfless? Isn't that very selfish?'

'When loving becomes as involuntary as your breathing - you would have reached the state where loving means simply existing, it is not done to reap any benefits. Would you still call it selfish?'

Down below, the sea roared its approval as waves splashed ferociously against the stones. In the room filled with gold and precious stones, what sparkled the brightest was his face.

Meera smiled and murmured, 'There could *not* be any other name for you. Sri Krsna, all-attractive one. If anyone can invoke such feelings, it's you.'

He smiled again. 'No, Meera. You can too if you are ready to submit yourself first.'

There ensued a silence except for the ecstatic cries of the sea.

'Everything and everyone has a purpose. Some realise it, some don't. Embodying that fearless love was the purpose of Rukmini's life. Giving the home to my people was the purpose of Dwarika.'

Meera had read how Yadavs had destroyed themselves towards the end, a tragedy attributed to Gandhari's curse, and how Dwarika had submerged following Krsna's demise. It gave her goose bumps to realise she was standing in that very ancient and glorious Dwarika and that too, in front of *Dwarikadheesh* himself. If she was hallucinating, so be it.

Love-something we all want, something we all chase knowingly or unknowingly and something we feel is dependent on someone else's mercy. But today Meera could feel that love was so much grander and deeper. She had understood Radha's unconditional love and now she was experiencing the love that Krsna inspired in Rukmini, the princess who let go of her *self* and ego to ask to be accepted and loved. Why can't people love like this anymore? Would she be able to love like this ever?

As she contemplated the newfound meaning of love, she realised her eyes were blurring. Brighter and brighter shone the room and a flash of light went out before Meera had to shut her eyes.

****

One can discern the darker darkness from the lighter darkness even when eyes are closed. That's what happened. Back in the mountains, Meera could feel the brightness of light with her closed eyelids and in astonishment, she opened her eyes. She was at the same rock where she had sat down to meditate. But in front she saw him - wearing the same shawl and *dhoti* and looking more majestic than ever. Meera lost all sense of time or place and was only aware of too much excitement and disbelief that hit her. She stood up in haste.

'Oh God, this is no longer a dream.'

'You did not really think it was a dream. You know better than that. You called me up.'

'Please don't ever abandon me.'

He laughed all of a sudden and it was a magnetic laughter. Somehow he both scared and comforted her. 'I never abandon those who seek me. Why did you call me?'

'I had no one else to go to. I didn't know who else could help me to find my lost peace of mind.'

'I accepted your devotion and plea for help. I showed you the path. And now it's up to you to be the God yourself.'

'Be the God?'

'Yes,' he said smiling. '*Tat Tvam Asi*. I am you and you are me. Awaken the God in yourself and you won't need to summon me again. But when you do, I will come.'

'How do I do that?'

'First - know that everything you perceive is an illusion. By the way, how do you like these mountains?'

'I love them. I feel I'm a part of them,' she replied gently.

'You both are a part of me, so you are not entirely wrong. Apart from that, they are here to just serve their purpose.'

'And what is their purpose?'

'These particular ones - to show the grandeur of life, to show how time can transform sediments into such massive formations, to show that there will always be something bigger than you.'

'You are taking their beauty away by putting it so objectively.'

He laughed again. 'Beauty is the worst of illusions. Don't love them for their beauty, love them for the purpose they serve.'

Meera ruminated on that and nodded.

'Talking of beauty, you might like this,' he said with a twinkle in his eyes that made Meera anticipate some kind of a miracle. It was a little cloudy where they were standing. As she looked around to discover what magic was about to unfold, the clouds parted to let the sun shine brighter. Meera was convinced that it was no coincidence. Before she could look back at him, she realised that the real miracle was something else: there were tens and hundreds of suns rising all around her in the sky until they flooded the sky with so much light that Meera could barely keep her eyes open.

'Holy crap,' came out the disbelief and she quickly apologised, 'I'm sorry. But this is insane. Please tell me this is not real.'

'Nothing is. That is exactly what I am telling you,' came the gentle reply. 'It could be hundred suns or green sky or four legged humans if that is what I wished.'

'Yes, Bhanudas told me too. It is just too fantastic to believe.'

He made the extra suns vanish and got the scenery back to its earlier form.

'So that was the first thing you need to understand. It is and will always be a virtual world. Don't let it sway you from your path. Love it or hate it but know it for what it is - an illusion.'

'I think I'll never forget it now.'

'Second - you have to perform your duties and realise your purpose. As I said, the river must not stop flowing even if it knows that the ocean is not the reality. As long as it exists, it needs to flow. Your duty towards the ones attached to you or dependent on you will always remain paramount. Performing your duty is another form of expressing your devotion.'

In front of Meera's eyes flashed the familiar faces of her parents, grandparents, close family and friends and Shimit.

'And life is my gift, those who try to destroy it can never find their purpose and peace.'

Her eyes lowered in shame as she gathered courage to assure him, 'I did learn my lesson and ever since that fateful night, I have valued every breath of mine. I can only tell you that I will not disappoint you again.'

'I hope you won't. And I hope you will value the other gift of mine too.'

She looked up questioningly, 'What is that?'

'Love. When living beings were created and granted senses that were sure to deceive them, it was decided to show them some mercy and they were given a power that would guide them in tough times. That power was the ability to love. It purifies the soul. Those who turn their backs to love struggle to find their truth. Loving is the only feeling worthy of your heart. Fill so much of it that there shall remain no space for desire, envy, greed, revenge or hatred.'

He continued, 'When you have practiced being comfortable with these two, aim for the third and last goal - whatever you do, do it with me in your heart and mind. Do it for me. And then nothing shall bind or affect you.'

'Is that what Bhanudas meant by dedicating the actions to you?'

'Yes. When I'm in your thoughts and consciousness, no karma shall ever affect you. That will happen when you reach the *superconscious stage - sthitaprajna*. Arjun asked me once -

*"Sthitaprajnasya kaa bhaashaa samaadhisthasya keshava;
Sthitadheeh kim prabhaasheta kimaaseeta vrajeta kim[39]"*

And this is what I told him

*"Prajahaati yadaa kaamaan sarvaan paartha manogataan;
Aatmanyevaatmanaa tushtah sthitaprajnastadochyate[40]"*

The key is '*Aatmanyevaatmanaa tushtah*' - it means focusing on one's *self*, letting yourself be content in *self*. You are too worried about the external world, the one that doesn't matter. What someone else will think of your choice shall not determine what you do. When you started following your calling and being content in yourself, you found yourself closer to me. Didn't you?'

Meera felt he was referring to her choice of pursuing photography.

'But it's not always easy to follow your calling. You did not design this world to facilitate that.'

'You are right, it is not easy. That is why only the ones with true

---

[39] What is the description of the man with a steady mind and who is merged in the super-conscious state?

[40] The one who is always content in the self by the self, is the one of steady wisdom.

calling can do it while others lose steam and get into the grind of illusions.'

'But my calling is eventually an illusion too. Even if I like photography and follow it, it will remain an illusion in your words.'

'Yes, but when you work towards your calling, your work transforms to love and faith that bring you closer to me.'

'What bothers me is that I will think everything is an illusion and I would want to give it all up. All I would care is to find you directly but you say that is not possible.'

'Some mortals did that and they were an exception. If you can do it, you will be another exception. That is a tougher road to walk but more glorious one.'

'Which is better?'

'Both and neither. Whether you come to me by performing your duties or renouncing everything, I welcome you with open arms. It is the realisation of your purpose that matters. What matters is that you understand that taste is an illusion and *okra* will taste exactly what you want it to taste like.'

Meera laughed for the first time in his presence and he smiled. And then Meera asked, 'Why did you create this illusion? I remember that ride in the enlightenment park where you showed me how it was all created. And, I wondered: why bother?'

'Because I could. And because it was one of my purposes.'

'Can I request something?'

'Yes.'

'Please help me so that I never go astray from the path you mentioned. And be my guardian so that I can attain my purpose.'

'I will. And I do it for most of the mortals but some are too busy to pay attention to my signals. I try to guide them through conscience, victories and losses, visions and love but besides that,

I let them make their own choices. And, sometimes I do test them too. I see if one gets swayed by worldly concerns - if losses unsettle them or if victories make them egoistic.'

'Will I see you again?'

'That is inevitable.'

And then his form started enlarging to kiss the sky itself. It grew till it engulfed the space around and then dissolved away. He was gone. She did not try to find him outside or inside, she just bowed her head down in reverence. She walked through the mountains watching the magnificent sunset again.

A year ago she could not have imagined reaching such a place in her life. Her whirlwind life stirred those forgotten essences that had precipitated to the bottom and she was now relishing their tastes. Chaos is fine, chaos is necessary to appreciate the need of order. Sitting in this pristine setting, she could think clearly and unveil her deeper layers. She came here to discover what lay within her and aided by the One, the complexities of life had unraveled.

At night she lit a small fire and sat by herself. She felt a peace and bliss she had never known before. She did think about Krsna and City of Justice again and again. She would miss those alleys and strange encounters, she thought. 'Perhaps, someday I'll get to be there again...' The fire crackled as she put small twigs and dry leaves into it. Her eyes watched the tangerine cores of the flames dancing in the mild air. In the USA, they loved to light fires in winters. Somehow in the warmth of fire, her whole journey of the past few years replayed before her eyes. And perhaps it was the warmth that filtered out the awful ones. She thought cozily of the big fireplaces they had in her school where she had sat down frequently to finish her homework. Her first phone call to her parents after reaching the USA and how much she had cried afterwards. She remembered her initial struggles in a foreign land. Surprisingly those were the strongest memories, after that it all faded until the painful ones started but she did not care about those anymore. Those struggles and scrambles of a new path define a person, they leave an indelible imprint on a person's journey, for one never really forgets them; they are the toughest to overcome and sweetest victories to relish later on.

She knew that one day she would fondly remember the lonely night when Krsna had first talked to her and smile at the day she had met him. Yes, this was another path and she would overcome the initial rough patches. It was not the road she had planned to take but a higher hand had intervened and she would follow it wherever it took her.

The gentle tread of footsteps broke her meditation as a girl came strolling from the nearby group of campers. 'How's your throat now?' she asked innocently. Meera felt embarrassed to have lied and said, 'It's better now.' Before she knew, she was coaxed into joining the campers for dinner and games. She was mostly silent but enjoyed the merry making of a group of strangers who celebrated in their blithe spirits. And soon, the fire extinguished, leaving behind smoke and ash; matter transforms from one form to another and so do we - physically and spiritually.

The night wore off quickly and a perfect sunrise rewarded her before the time came to return. Her first rendezvous with the Himalayas had made her a believer in no time. After all they had facilitated her first real divine encounter. She looked around at the mountains, forest, sky and the water with admiration. She felt as if she could now talk to them and the wind - they were unified in their existence for a purpose. She had discovered that she already knew their language; she just didn't know that she knew it - the cosmos made her aware of that. And the resounding reply she heard back was 'tat tvam asi' - that thou are - your divine self is inseparable from the One. 'We are the drops of the same ocean,' was the farewell message from the Himalayas to Meera.

As she descended, she knew that the real challenge did not lie in finding the inner peace but maintaining it once she went back to the chaos of city and daily life. She would need to practice the secret of the restraint she had successfully learned, and keep controlling the inner clamor. Lastly, she was no longer afraid of being hurt and she had decided to open herself up to true love. Love is more than ego.

****

In the train ride on her way back, she pulled out the small journal from her knapsack.

Dear Diary,

I met Him and He told me the secret-

I am Brahma, the cosmic force and the ultimate truth. I am Him and He is me. I exist in His divine existence and He exists in mine. Aham Brahmasmi.

To feel defeated is to accept His defeat. To let myself sink is to sink Him. He has restored me and shows me the path ahead when I leave myself on His mercy. Where else would I go when He is breathing within me?

-Meera

Chapter TWENTY-SIX
The Call

It had been a week since her return from the eventful excursion. She was in the garden. The paint tubes lay carelessly on an artist table next to a big standing easel that held a tall canvas.

Meera was squinting at a delicate line she was painting with her size zero filbert at the precise moment when her cell phone's raucous ringtone broke her concentration. She hastily pinned the brush in her messy hair knot to answer it.

'Hello.'

'Hi Kiddo!'

Meera's heart skipped a beat before answering, 'Shimit! How are you?'

She could hear him smiling at the other end.

'The war threat is over.'

Her eyes closed tightly in relief as she slumped down on the ground. Her hand clutched the phone harder.

'So yeah, I'm good but I'm starving.'

She smiled while her moist eyes blinked fast, 'Just come, this time I'll cook.'

'Great, just what I wanted to hear.'

She felt she was being awfully quiet and that she should say something, 'I'm so happy to hear your voice.'

'You better be because I am coming for a long vacation now.'

'I can't wait.'

'Me too. See you then.'

'See you.'

Meera looked at her canvas. The unfinished painted peacock feather seemed to be fluttering.

****

63830832R00132

Made in the USA
Middletown, DE
05 February 2018